Lily Darling

a novella by Malesha Smith

Lily Darling

A novella by Malesha Smith

Copyright © January 22, 2020 Malesha Smith
Cover photograph: Mikayla Smith

A Meredith *Etc* Book
Meredith *Etc*
1052 Maria Court
Jackson, MS 39204-5151
www.meredithetc.com

First printing - Softcover edition
Black & white interior
Printed by Kindle Direct Publishing
ISBN-13: 978-0-9993226-9-7
115 pages

Hardback edition
ISBN-13: 978-1-7341578-0-2
Printed by Ingram Press

ISBN-13: 978-1-7341578-5-7
Printed by Barnes & Noble Press

Available on the World Wide Web as an eBook

Keywords: Novella, Lily Mitchell, bullying, self-esteem, middle school, Mississippi writer

DEDICATION

The book is for my five children and all the children around the world who shed unmerited tears because of the degrading words or actions of their peers and others.

CONTENTS

ACKNOWLEDGMENTS

First, I thank Almighty God for everything He has done for me and for everything He has been to me throughout my life. Without His grace, this book could not become a reality.

I would like to thank my children (my 5 Heartbeats), Mikayla, Brianna, Jayeden, Haleigh, and Chelsea for the outpouring of love and support. Questions such as *"Mom, are you finished with your book yet?"* would be asked at the most opportune moments and sometimes would be the deciding factor between giving up and finishing. Their anticipation and excitement from the very first day pushed me to complete this project and will forever be written in my heart. I am proud to be their mom.

I'd like to thank the father and mother of Warrior Nation, Mr. and Mrs. Sino and Kellie Agueze. For it was they who said, *"Your purpose is when your pain and your passion intercepts."* From that moment, I knew I had to share this story. I am one warrior whose life has been forever changed.

I sincerely thank my friends Krissie Sago, Tiara Wilson, Nakeisha Pinkston for every encouraging word and act of kindness and support they displayed throughout this journey. No words can express how grateful I am. I would also like to thank all my family for everything.

I am greatly indebted to my publisher and editor Meredith Coleman McGee for guiding me through this foreign process of publishing a book. Her expertise is greatly appreciated.

Finally, I give a special thank you to every person who has talked about me, who has ever made me cry, made me feel less than, or made my children feel this way; you are truly appreciated. Now I know that you, too, were part of the plan.

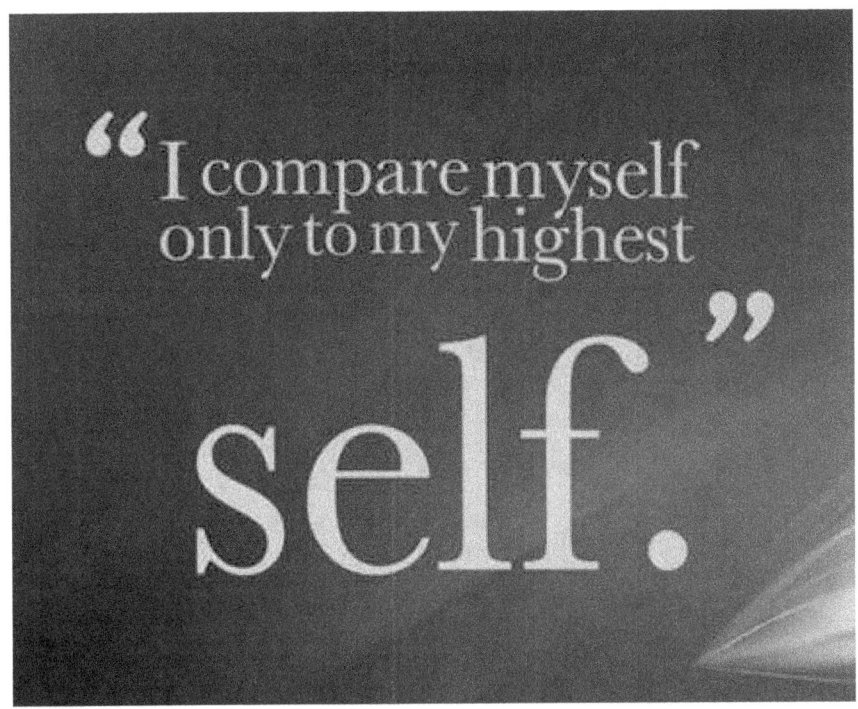

"I compare myself only to my highest self."

Lily Darling, a novella by Malesha Smith

One in five USA school pupils are bullied nationally. Lily Mitchell, the main character, a Langley Middle School student, is subjected to the harmful behavior of bullies. The negative forces of bullies caused Lily to abhor the image of herself in the mirror, her bus ride to school, and her existence on the school landscape.

A new girl at school, Jerica, gradually brings balance to Lily's existence by teaching her the principles of positive reaffirmation. One day Lily pulled Julius, a stranger, from the butt end of a tiger fight in an alleyway. In the end, can Lily and Jerica save Julius?

https://meredithetc.com/lily-darling/ *Lily Darling* – webpage

CHAPTER 1

Don't Let Them See You Cry

7:00 a.m.

It takes everything in me not to reach over and hit the snooze button on the alarm clock again as it rings for the second time this morning. But, I'm pretty sure I'll be late if I do. So, I decide against prolonging the inevitable. I turn on my back and stare at the ceiling fan. I drift off to sleep momentarily only to be awaken from the sounds of my own snoring. I shift my body to the left and let my feet hang on the side of my bed.

7:05 a.m.

This Monday starts off like any other typical school day as I stand in my closet contemplating what to wear. I don't care how many times I tell myself to pick out my school clothes the night before, I never do. Every school morning, I find myself back in the closet staring at the same clothes, waiting for an outfit to put itself together. Sometimes I pretend I'm a witch as I twirl and swirl my fingers around hoping to ignite some deeply buried magical power. My supernatural powers haven't worked, yet; but hey there's no harm in trying.

My complicated process of selecting an outfit to wear to school wouldn't be necessary if I lived in a world free from judging. Picking an outfit would be easy, if I could pick any old shirt laying around, some jogging pants, and a comfortable pair of slide-ins. The process would be simple and comfortable, just how I like it. The way I see it, school is already hard enough; going through the pain of trying to find an outfit that makes me look thinner is almost impossible. However, in this day and age, I wouldn't dare be caught wearing the wrong color panties let alone an entire outfit.

I finally go with a pair of stonewashed, skinny jeans and all gray Converses complimented by a turquoise raglan, Mickey Mouse top. It isn't my sweats and slide-ins, but it will have to do. Plus, it happens to be my second favorite outfit.

7:15 a.m.

My heart pounds harder than normal as I stare at the digital clock sitting on the nightstand in my bedroom. I search frantically for my book bag and my jacket. It's only after throwing my clothes all over my bedroom floor that I suddenly remember my mom telling me she put them both in her bedroom closet. I had inadvertently left them in her car when she took off work Friday after I pretended to be sick. Although I hate lying to my mom, I just couldn't muster up enough energy to endure another moment at school.

It was one of those days when everything seemed to go wrong. Before my feet hit the ground, I was already defeated. Days like that, I wish I could sleep away just to escape the prison inside my head where my thoughts keep me captive. Thoughts

2

that constantly tells me that I'm not good enough and convinces me that my existence isn't important. Maybe it was the strain of that day that caused me to forget where my belongings were. Or maybe it was karma doing what karma does best, biting me in the butt at the most inopportune time for lying to my mom about being sick.

7:18 a.m.

Maybe, I'll have time to get to the bus stop before the other students arrive. I run outside with my book bag and jacket in tow. My heart goes from pounding louder than an African tribal drum session, to dead silence as my heart stops beating for a moment. I glance at the gathered crowd of students at the bus stop. Everyone is accounted for and to make things worse, the twins who rarely ride the bus are here bright and early this morning. Zoe and Cam are identical twin brother and sister. Cam plays on the Jr. Varsity basketball team. Zoe mostly keeps to herself usually with a novel of some sort in her hand. They are a year older than me in the eighth grade. Both are pretty cool, but I absolutely hate when they decide to ride the bus instead of getting dropped off by their parents. They only catch the bus, on an average, about twice a week and if I'm really lucky less than that. Obviously, today is not my lucky day.

The twins and I have never had any falling out. But when they ride the bus, they sort of make my life a living hell because it means they occupy two seats, on an already overly packed bus, that could have possibly been mine. This usually means that I am left walking the Green Mile. The Green Mile consists of me drudgingly walking down the aisle of the bus asking one student after another if I can sit down. As I walk toward the group, the twins speak to me in unison above the chattering of the other kids standing around.

I wave my hand to greet them. In the same moment, I can hear the squealing of brakes as our school bus approaches. The

3

flashing yellow and red lights are already on as the stop sign springs out and the door opens. I watch all the other students at the bus stop climb up the steps of the bus ahead of me and I can only hope that there's an available seat left. If not, I won't only have to hear the self-absorb, tormenting pricks tell me I can't sit down, but I'll also have to hear them go into vivid details as to why. I swear some of the stuff they say is crazy but somehow it has me questioning myself.

I've heard that I'm too fat to sit down with them and that I would take up the whole seat. So, now when I sit down, I try to keep my body from touching whoever I'm sitting with which is a very difficult task because Mr. Harrison, our bus driver, drives like he's auditioning for a gig on Grand Theft Auto. I've also been told that I stank of cat litter, which is important to notate that I don't own any pet, let alone a cat. So, I started showering in the morning and using some of my mom's Victoria Secret to guarantee freshness.

I always took my shower at night but maybe somehow, I was secreting bodily fluids that made an odor in my sleep. Yeah, incredulous I know but the persistent slandering of these bullies has made me take extra measures. However, I quickly learned that a fresh bath in the morning and some very good smelling perfume was not going to stop the constant belittling that these aliens dish out every morning. I call them aliens because there's no way any human could be so mean. Again, the bullying is the reason I wish the twins had rode to school with their parents. They take the little chance I had to secure a seat of my own with someone who doesn't think making someone feel lower than dirt is cool.

As I get on the bus, I try to muster up as much courage as I can. But as I look from the front of the bus to the back of the already crowded bus, the little hope I hang on to disappears quickly. Every step down the Green Mile feels like a little bit of life is taking from me. I see the twins sitting together all cozy at the front of the bus and I shake my head in disappointment

4

regretting not getting up the first time the alarm went off.

The first seat available belongs to Michelle Latiker, who sits alone toward the middle of the bus. Michelle is an obnoxious seventh grader whose arrogance enters a room before she steps foot in the room herself. You would think with such high self-esteem that she would be extremely beautiful. But truth be told, Michelle is mediocre to say the least. She's noticeably frail, with thinning shoulder length hair. She wears her clothes tighter than necessary as if she is trying to produce assets, she doesn't possess by squeezing them into existence. Her face is covered with enough acne which would have made her a perfect model for a Proactive commercial. The only thing more concerning than her unusual skinniness would be how long her feet are. She almost looks like a walking and talking stick figure whose illustrator got a little heavy handed when it came to drawing her feet.

I start to walk pass her, but I thought it wouldn't hurt to ask. Maybe she's feeling extra friendly today. I open my mouth to ask if I can sit. Before a single word comes out, she glares at me and turn sideways. Now with her back pressing against the window, she props up one of her legs on the empty portion of the seat. Clearly stating, without words, she didn't want me to sit with her.

Slowly, I tread on. My eyes dart from left to right hoping with all hopes that a seat will magically appear from thin air to no avail. I approach Desmond Snider's seat. Desmond is a seventh grader with a chip on his shoulder. Maybe the fact that he is the only 15-year-old in the same grade with 13-year-olds has a lot to do with it. Either way, he is abnormally mean to be so incredibly dumb. And I'm not saying this to be offensive, but I overheard him on several occasions having conversations that were dang near incoherent. I haven't heard so many subject-verb disagreements, and inappropriate verb tenses before in my life. What makes it worse, is the fact that he talks about everybody and their momma.

This time he was picking on another student that I didn't recognize. "You gots so many mouses in yours house that they sits at the kitchen table for dinner with yalls." You would've thought I was watching one of those movies where someone from a foreign country comes to the United States learning to speak English for the first time. I can only imagine how proud his English teachers must be.

"Hey Desmond, can I sit with you?" I blurted out. It was still worth a try.

"Now why would I let a fat soma wrestler sit with me and squeeze me to death? Besides, you would probably have me smelling like a pissy cat before I make it to school." Desmond says loudly as some of the students on the bus begin to laugh.

There it was. The moment I dreaded the most. Contrary to the familiar phrase, "*Sticks and stones may break my bones, but words will never hurt me,*" I was injured, nevertheless. Every word that he spat out hurt like a thousand paper cuts slicing through my self-esteem, my self-worth, and my confidence. I begin to gasp for breath as the words begin to suffocate me with sadness. Tears begin to well up behind my eyelids and with one blink I know I won't be able to contain them any longer before they start to stream down my face.

Breathe, Lily. Just breathe.

My mom always told me, no *matter what, don't let them see you cry.* I plan to honor this as I walk toward the front of the bus and get off. The moment both feet touch the ground, the tears flow like the gushing waters of Niagara Falls. Walking towards the front door of my house, I was sure not to turn around. *Don't let them see you cry Lily. Don't let them see you cry.*

By the time my well of tears finally dries up, it's too late for me to walk to school without having someone sign me in. Since

I hate bothering my mom at work and I don't want to go anyway; the decision to stay at home is easy. I'll just have to be careful not to leave the house in a mess, so my mom won't think anything is out of the ordinary.

As I walk around the empty house, memories of my Pawpaw flood my mind. He was one of the funniest men I've ever met. If he was still alive today, he would be sitting on the front porch wearing his farmer john's blue jean overalls with a button-down flannel shirt. Ohh,' how I miss that man. A day like this would be spent fixing or building something around the house. He loved staying busy. Every time you looked around, he'd be saying something needs to be fixed. Squeaky doors, broken cabinets, even a broken umbrella, it didn't matter as long as he had something to do. And you could find me sitting excitedly by his side with no worries or no fear. No matter what I was going through outside this house, I always felt complete whenever I was with him. But now that he's gone, I struggle daily to find my place in this world.

I grab the throw blanket laying on the living room couch and walk toward the old, worn out recliner near the window. It was Paw-Paw's favorite chair. My mom tried to get rid of it when he passed but I pleaded with her to let me keep it. I needed to keep something that I could remember him by. Days like these, I'm glad I fought so hard against removing the chair as I curl up under the blanket. Distant memories of shared laughter and love played in my mind as peaceful thoughts consoled me to sleep.

"Lily, I know you heard me the first time. You can come down to eat."

"Okay, I'm on my way now," I shouted loud enough for my mom to hear. I heard her the first time but after waking up from my much-needed nap earlier, I dedicated the rest of my day to watching movies. I was in the middle of a really great one and I didn't care to ruin the moment by joining mama for dinner. Which says a lot since lunch has secured a number one spot on the list of my favorite subjects in school for as long as I can remember.

Watching movies has become a norm for me. I love watching complete strangers act out a knowingly false reality. I enjoy journeying through their lives experiencing the sorrow of heart breaks and despair and rejoicing in the moments of happiness and victory as if their lives were my very own. My soul becomes intertwined with every character I watch. Somehow, I become one with every one of them. And for the short duration of the film, I am lost to my own reality to be caught up in new adventures, new experiences, and new people.

For this brief time, I take a break from being Lillian Mitchell. Willingly swapping lives with Captain Jack Sparrow living carelessly on the Perl seeking unknown lands for unfounded treasures. I live the life of Cinderella, as I journey the paths of overcoming hardships and adversity at such a young age, but fate inevitably leads me down the path of happiness. I become one with Katniss Everdeen as uncontrollable circumstances forces me to dig deep within myself searching for strength and power to become a person I never thought I could be.

I've lived many lives, across many lands and have experienced pain to depths of unbelief but it never fails that happiness always follows in close pursuit behind every turn. I fall in love with chivalrous men that adore the very ground I walk on. As the characters brave wars of inner demons and fears, I too inhibit this newly founded strength and confidence.

But this only occurs when I am taking afar in the world of make believe. It is only in these moments that I can escape the turmoil that my life brings. Feelings of worthlessness and hopelessness that tears me apart mentally. The feeling of numbness that I can't fully comprehend. Neither can I find the words to even express to others, the feelings of despair that has become a dark shadow that hovers over me day in and day out.

It's like falling into a deep, dark, hole and no matter how hard I try, I can't seem to get out of it. I try to strike a match so I can see myself out the abyss, but the darkness engulfs me. I try to climb out of it aimlessly to no avail. The only solace I find is watching these movies. But as the closing threads come flashing down the television screen, the painstaking realities of what is called my life rushes back in like a flood.

The sweet aroma of seasoning, spices, and herbs of spaghetti sauce filled the air as soon as I reached the top of the stairs. The day is pasta night in the Mitchell's household. Planning out meals is a habit of my moms to keep down expenses and stress levels by eliminating the constant questioning of what is on the menu every night.

The only down fall from planned meals is that it's a guarantee that I will have to eat beans at least 52 times a year because Wednesday is the dreadful bean day. And I hate beans. Pinto, black-eyed, kidney, it doesn't matter. All beans suck. But living with a mom like mine it's either take it or leave it. Most of the time, I take it. But GYO (Get Your Own) Thursdays makes up for it all. That's when I can pick out whatever I want to eat just if I cook. Thursday's are my mom's vacation days from cooking because she swears cooking is a job all within itself.

Planning meals was something her mother and her grandmother did faithfully. They instilled in her that a planned-out day will go smoother than just going with the flow, often leaving some wiggle room to manage when an unexpected crisis hit. A good plan is always accompanied by great timing. A saying that is often heard in the Mitchell's household especially when I, a naturally born procrastinator, will put off almost any task gifted to me. Thus, the reason why I hurriedly clump down the stairs trying to beat the third beckoning from my mother that would assuredly be followed with a lecture about arriving on time.

"I called you down twice Lily. If this was a job interview, you would have undoubtedly made a bad first impression. Who would want to hire a person who's late?" Here we go again. Only my mom can draw a connection between being late for dinner and work ethics.

"Sorry mom, I just wanted to finish the movie before I ate." I replied, instantly regretting not coming up with a more acceptable reason to be late for dinner.

"What have I told you about prioritizing your time, Lily Bug?" mama asked not expecting a response.

"You can watch a movie in your spare time. But I cook dinner at a specific time to ensure you have enough time to eat, do the dishes, take a bath, and get back into bed so that you can get 8 hours of sleep at night."

"I know mom, that's why I finished my homework for the whole week and after getting done I decided to watch a movie. I thought it would have been over before dinner." I added for good measure, hoping she would appreciate that I didn't dally around to the last minute on my homework as usual. Even though homework only consisted of a list of words and their definitions I looked up to study since it was testing all week long at Langley Middle School. A small detail I was careful to leave out.

"Okay," my mom nodded her head with approval.

"While I'm thinking about it, did you sign up for the talent show? If I recall correctly, the last day to sign up is next Thursday, right?"

Crap, not the talent show again, I think silently. At that very same moment, the telephone rings. And the interruption couldn't have come at a better time for me. My mom has been pushing me to start being involved in more extracurricular school activities. I am totally against participating in school activities and joining clubs. It is no secret that I am not the most popular person at school. You can survey the entire student body but only a select few know Lillian Mitchell.

Being unknown is fine with me. Out of the limelight and hiding behind the shadows of the walls is normal to me. Out of sight, out of mind. In fact, if it had been left up to me, I would have been home-schooled years ago. With the many benefits of homeschooling growing by the minute, it's a wonder why all parents (mainly mine) haven't jumped on this opportunity.

Academic flexibility, meaningful learning environments, meeting current needs, and choice of pace and approach are perks of home schooling. Check, check, check, and check. And 'home schools' are at home which is away from the critical eye of my peers. Double check. Everything about homeschooling makes perfect sense to me, sentiments I shared by writing a one-page essay that I presented to my mom two years ago. My mom did not quit her job and turn our den into a school. Nevertheless, presenting the essay to her was worth a shot.

My mom, who is only partially aware of the daily struggles I am experiencing at school, believes that my lack of social involvement plays a big part in my overall confidence level. However, I can't see how joining a group filled with students who don't understand me, like me, or care to try to like me would boost my self-esteem. So, after months of being badgered by my mother, it sort of slipped out that the school was showcasing a talent show that I may enter, even though I had no real intention of signing up. It was just something to get my mom off my back. What seemed like a good idea at first, turned into constant suggestions of what I could do in the talent show and about 20 stories on what she sung at her elementary school's talent show and how she landed second place out of two contestants.

Mom answered the phone. "Hello, Mrs. Cooper...... No, we were just sitting down for dinner.... Yes, would you like to speak to her? It's for you. It's Mrs. Cooper." she said handing me the phone.

"Hey, Mrs. Cooper. How are you?" my tone goes up an octave. Partially because I'm always excited to talk with her and partially so she can hear me better. Mrs. Cooper is 65-years old but from the way she looks and acts you wouldn't suspect it. Her mind is sharper than a double-edged razor and her tongue is even sharper. I've been knowing her practically my whole life. Ever since my mom and I moved into the neighborhood seven years ago, she has lived right around the corner from us.

In fact, everybody in the neighborhood knows her because she's the Candy Lady. All the little children pimp their mom out of money daily just to spend it at Mrs. Cooper's snack shop.

Snickers. M&Ms. Skittles. Airheads. Doritos, Flammin' Hots, and Takis. And for some extra change you can get some hot cheese drizzled on top of it.

Hot dogs. Kool-Aid pickles. Boiled Peanuts. You name it, she has it.

And don't let me forget my favorite. Icee Cups which is Kool-Aid, frozen in a cup that's so sweet you get Type 2 Diabetes from staring at it hard.

She sales single Newport's for 50 cents and she keeps a box of mini Swisher Sweets that she sells for a dollar each.

"Hey, girlie." Mrs. Cooper hollered through the phone. For some reason, she couldn't grasp the concept that she didn't have to talk any louder just because she was on the phone. "I thought you said you were coming over after school to help me finish cleaning up the bedroom before my granddaughter gets here. Now I may be old and partially blind, but I know I haven't seen your black butt over here today."

Dang, I had completely forgotten. She had asked me last week to spend a couple of hours after school to finish cleaning up the spare bedroom that was now the home of her many books and other items she had collected from flea markets and yard sales, a hobby that had grown uncontrollably in the last couple of years since her husband died. The death of Mr. Cooper left a void in

Mrs. Cooper that she constantly tries to fill by keeping herself as busy as possible which includes purchasing all kinds of unnecessary junk. I can see hoarder listed as a job description on her resume.

"I'm so sorry, Mrs. Cooper. It totally slipped my mind. But I will be there tomorrow to help around the house. I should be there around 3:30 if that works for you?"

"Yeah, that will work. Now don't come by tomorrow. I'll be making a special visit over there to come see about you. Maybe then, you'll get your act right."

I swear Mrs. Cooper talks cash money bull.

"No need for all that, I'll be there tomorrow for sure." I hang up the phone.

"Forgot to do something that you gave your word to do?" Mama asked already knowing the answer. "Maybe now you'll use that planner I bought you three months ago that you haven't even bothered to put your name in. I've told you a thousand times a good plan is always—"

"Always accompanied by great timing." I finished the sentence for her.

"So, what are you doing for Mrs. Cooper?" mom asked.

"I'm cleaning up the spare room before her granddaughter gets here."

"Oh, that must be Julie's daughter. I've heard she's been going through a rough patch lately and that sweet innocent daughter of hers has been bouncing around from one place to another. I'm glad to hear she's coming here to stay with Mrs. Cooper. It'll be good for her. Maybe you two will be friends."

Friends?

Maybe.

I doubt it though. I haven't made a friend after this long and I don't see that's about to change now.

CHAPTER 2

The New Girl

The walk to school on a warm August morning like today is not so bad. However, walking to school means I'll miss breakfast which is no small price to pay; but, avoiding the unpleasantness on the bus is better than facing the jeering students. At least I can gather my thoughts and enjoy the scenery for the time being. But peace and quiet will only last the short duration of the walk because as soon as I step foot into Langley Middle School everything is different. For some reason, as I walk through the halls, I feel like all eyes are on me. Not just regular eyes that see but eyes that talk and yes, eyes that scrutinize every inch of me.

The eyes examine my clothes, my shoes, my height, my weight, and my existence. The eyes judge me, compare me to themselves, and form opinions about me without even knowing me. Then, those same eyes begin to label me and categorize me, putting me in a group. Contrary to how the students of Hogwarts are placed in houses based on their patience, bravery, chivalry, wits, and creativity.

These eyes see my full figure and say:

She's not skinny. Her hips are broad; her shoulders are wide; her legs are long; her arms are long; her feet are big; her fingers are long. She is different; she is made funny; let's laugh; let's laugh hard; let's laugh boldly; let's treat her coldly. See, I will pick on her. Watch me pick on her. Laugh! Look at me. Look at her. Laugh! Did you hear me? Did you see her. She feels badly. I did it. Yes, I did it. I made her little. I am big. Laugh! Laugh! Laugh! Laugh!

These eyes look at my skin complexion and say I'm not light enough. These eyes look at my hair and say it isn't long enough. Eyes that aren't meant to talk have the power to speak negativity that creates an unseen cloud which hovers over me. Unseen but not unheard. *She's too fat… She's ugly… Why does she have those type of shoes on?* Nope, not unheard at all. Whispers can clearly be heard throughout the atmosphere and just like that without getting to know who I am, how I treat people, or what I stand for, I am labeled an outcast. Arriving just seconds before the last bell rings to get to my homeroom class goes off, I hurriedly take my seat at the front of the class. My desk is directly in front of Michelle's. I feel her beady eyes pierce into my back as I take my notebook out of my book bag.

"Ugh, why did she have to come to school?" Michelle asks disgustedly, to no one in particular, but clearly wanting me to know how displeased she was to see me. (Because this is a public school that you don't own. Looking like the seed of Chucky with your thinning hair. I swear one of these days I'm going to snap on one of these fools).

I extract my pencil and my science study questions from my bag pretending I didn't hear her. Suddenly, Mr. Stone, my homeroom and science teacher walks in. The room instantly quiets down. Everybody knows Mr. Stone, an army veteran and current head coach of the boys' basketball team, doesn't play.

16

Peering over his glasses, he scans the room as if in search of someone. Following his eyes, I see them land on a girl I've never seen before sitting in the far-right corner of the classroom. With a nod of acknowledgement, Mr. Stone clears his voice to get the attention of the class.

"Okay guys, we have a new student with us today. Everyone let's welcome Jerica Thompson. She'll be joining us for the rest of the school year."

All eyes are now on Jerica. Some of the class whispers almost inaudible hellos. But she doesn't seem to mind all the probing eyes. Kudos to her because I don't really know what I would have done in her position. Most likely my anxiety would have gotten the best of me and I would have just hung my head and shut my mouth. But Jerica throws a wiggly wave and flashes a half smile toward the class and looks back up to Mr. Stone as if having the entire classroom looking at her was normal.

And as on cue, Mr. Stone announces in his deepest authoritative voice, "Students please take out your science guide and turn to chapter two." Just like that, Jerica is out of the spotlight and everything continues as usual. How does she do it? Not the least bothered by one soul in this room.

I've seen quite a few new students over the years and the ones that seem to naturally fit in are the spoiled cheerleader type or the arrogant football player. Although, Jerica wasn't ugly by any means, she didn't fit into the spoiled, bratty, 'I think I'm all that' category. She isn't small, but not big either. Her butterscotch complexion with her hair secured sleekly in a ponytail at the nape of her neck, made her looked older but youthful at the same time. She sported a slightly oversized sweater paired with black leggings and a pair of red and white Jordan Retro 11; her outfit screamed, 'I wear what I want to wear.'

She wasn't a Black Barbie. Yet, she still held the pretty girl, calm and collected demeanor. She did not appear bothered by what people think about her. It's almost as though she was Beyoncé and we were her Beehive. Everything about her exudes confidence. I'm truly impressed, and my eyes follow her the entire class period. Awkwardly, I get caught a couple of times, but I had become mesmerized by her grace and poise. And I'm not the only one. Desmond's eyes were focused intently on the new girl. He was quiet as a mouse. He didn't pass any notes. He didn't drop his pen on the floor. Nothing.

"Who wants to read and answer the question to number 5?" Mr. Stone asked scanning the room for volunteers.

Desmond Snider raised his hand and swirled two of his index fingers in the air. "Me. Me. I'll read it Mr. Stone." He was leaning halfway out of his desk with his arms raised high while moving them from side to side, anxiously trying to get Mr. Stone's attention. The gesture was a little over the top since he was the only one with his hands up. Murmuring of protest spread throughout the class as always when Desmond volunteered to read.

"Come on now, Dez." Rico Greene shouted from the back of the classroom. You can clearly hear the frustration in his voice. For the life of me or anyone else in my classroom, we couldn't figure out why he always wanted to read when reading was clearly not his strong point. Yet, Desmond is always eager to nominate himself for the task whenever he got a chance and regrettably, we would have to endure the excruciating, drawn out minutes it took him to stutter over simple words as he tried to get his sentences completed. And each time would be quickly followed by a big, wide, Cheshire cat smile as if he had done us a favor by gracing us with his reading.

His reading level was no laughing matter to me. It was a poor reflection of, not only, Desmond but the school, the teachers, and his parents. Personally, I feel like someone should be held accountable. Not simply because he reads poorly because I have studied other students and have come to the realization that we all learn differently. Some students are naturally smart. They just get it. A lot of students are like me who can understand a lot of the material being given to us but must put in a lot of work like studying, researching, and asking questions just to keep our heads above water. And then there are students like Desmond who learns slower than most. Sometimes because he doesn't apply himself but most of the time because he has reached his capacity. I blame the higher ups for not intervening and investing in Desmond's intellectual growth.

With that being said, I still don't understand how in the world Desmond Snider can talk about anybody. How can a person with their own shortcomings look at me and feel like they can judge mine? I don't get bullying. I will never understand how anyone on this earth can talk about anybody because we're all so different. How can anyone feel like they're better than the others when there is so much variety in the world? I still haven't found an answer to this.

Finally, the bell rings for us to change classes. Gathering my belongings, I head out the door when I feel someone grab my arm. Turning on my heels, I look to see who is holding on to me.

"I'm sorry but I didn't know how to get your attention." Jerica said abruptly letting go of her grip.

"You're good." shrugging my shoulders, I move further in the hallway to let the other students past us since we were standing inside the doorway of the classroom.

"I was wondering if you could show me to my classes today, assuming we are taking the same classes."

Of all the students in the class she chooses me to ask about her classes. I must say, I would've been genuinely honored to just sit next to her but to actually talk to me and ask me to take her somewhere. I'm lost for words.

I don't know why she picked me; but in doing so she sparked something in me. My overly active imagination is in full speed. Maybe she is one of the few people, like me, who picks up on people's vibes. Maybe she is being drawn to me by an unseen force which would lead to a new and very much needed friendship since finding true friendship is such a rarity for me.

My last so-called friend was actually pretty cool. Nicole Baxter accepted me for who I am. I never had to pretend to be something I wasn't. Everything was fine and dandy until one day, out of the blue, she starts hanging out with Michelle. I never felt so betrayed in my entire life. Not that Nicole treated me bad or anything, but how could she want to befriend such a terrible person like Michelle was mind-boggling. And Michelle isn't a good friend either.

She talks about Nicole in front of her face and behind her back. Nicole always laughs it off, but I can't stand how she's always picking on her. It's not Nicole's fault her eyebrows are so light that it blends into her skin making it look like she doesn't have any hair above her eyes. Michelle also has a habit of calling Nicole out her name just to get laughs from other students. How she can stand someone to belittle and humiliate her just to fit in is something I could never understand or accept. Nicole's inability to see that her so-called friendship with Michelle was nothing close to friendly is the reason why Nicole and I are no longer friends. If she can't stand up for herself, there's no way I could expect her to stand up for me.

"Let me see your schedule." I said, reaching for the piece of paper Jerica was holding in her hand. "If you're in my homeroom we'll be taking the same classes with the exception of electives depending on what you choose."

"Well, I haven't decided yet. I told the counselor that I wanted to explore my options before I decided."

I scoffed a little trying to hold back laughter at the word options, "Well we only have P.E., band, and performing arts. So, it all depends on whether you are a physical person, a music person, or artistry. Actually, the performing arts program is fairly, new. Adding it to the curriculum may have had a lot to do with people like me who hate dressing out in shorts sweating all over the place and like listening to music but not actually playing an instrument."

"So, I'm assuming you are taking performing arts," Jerica looked pensively as though she was thinking it over in her head.

I nod my head forward and backward indicating 'yes.'
"What do you do in performing arts class?"

"Well, we write poems and short stories. We also produce musical plays."

"Do you perform in front of an audience?"

"Some students do but me I just like to do the minimum like setting up the stage, working with costumes, and props. Nothing in the spotlight."

Well, that isn't entirely true. I would like to dance. No, I would love to dance. Not your typical street dance but dancing that comes from the soul, almost like praise dancing in the church.

Dancing is something I learned to appreciate last summer after hearing *Ready for Love* by India Arie for the first time. My mom always listens to old school R&B around the house and in the car. She believes the music of this day and time has no substance. And for the longest time, I dismissed her as another old head hating on the younger generation's music for no other reason except, she is getting old. Ever heard the saying, *if you can't beat them, hate on them?*

But the moment I heard that song, I was forever changed. It explores depths of love that I couldn't have ever imagined. And yes, I may be young but even 13-year-olds have an opinion of what love is. Sure, young love may be wet behind the ears and a little naïve. And it may not need to be explored until later when life has chewed us up and spat us out. But wanting to share your life with someone who unequivocally loves you is seeded at birth.

Every word of that song speaks volumes. But words weren't enough, I felt it needed to be expressed with the body. That day, I twirled across my bedroom floor as graceful as a dandelion blown in the spring wind. The connection my soul made to the lyrics of that song through dance was an encounter I couldn't explain. Freedom. It felt like I was being lifted into another realm and peace met me at its open door. I was on a high that I didn't want to come down from. And since then, I find myself longing to reach that high over-and-over again.

"Sounds good enough for me, I'll tell the counselor that I'll take performing arts as my elective. So, we're off to our math class, right?" she asked taking hold of her schedule again.

"Yes, we are." Desmond chimes in before I can answer.

"I'm just wondering why you want Lillian fat ass to take you when I would be more than happy to walk you myself."

Here we go again. As if the spectacle on the bus yesterday morning wasn't enough already. Slowly, I bow my head down not knowing what else to do as my fantasies of a new founded friendship ends. It is one thing to talk about me but to talk about me in front of Jerica is an entirely different level of humiliation. You see, Jerica is new; she doesn't know that I am the most devalued about person in the entire school or that I don't have friends. She doesn't know all the hurtful things people say about me.

It's like going to a new school where no one knows you. Your slate is wiped clean and you find yourself liked by everybody at this new school. Right when you start feeling a sense of belonging, someone from the past comes along and starts the same old crap that you just escaped from the old school. Now, you start to see those same people who just started to take a liking to you switch up on you. Boom, just like that, you are right back to square one: an outcast.

So, I'm not as mad at Desmond for calling me fat but for him extinguishing any glimmer of hope of having a friendship with someone like Jerica. I couldn't muster enough courage to look at Jerica. I was too afraid of what her facial expression would tell me. If she couldn't look me in the eyes, that would mean she took what Desmond said and decided it best not to associate with someone like me.

If she looks like she is smiling, she'd probably find me being the butt of an amusing joke. If she didn't do either and she still wanted to befriend me, then… Then, I wouldn't know what that would look like since I had little experience with friendship. Either way, I refuse to set myself up for failure. What can I say? I am ashamed and I can't shake the feeling no matter how hard I try. I hate when I get like this too.

Normally, I would just start replaying the scene back in my head but instead of walking away when Desmond calls me fat, I would have a comeback like, *I know I may not be your fun size Snicker but trust me when I say that king size is just as good.* And then I'd imagine everybody would laugh and pat me on the back and tell me how crazy I am. Or just as soon as he calls me fat, I ball my fat hand, and swing my fat arm until it makes contact with his fat mouth resulting in a fat lip. Again, everybody roots me on and tells Desmond that's what he gets for popping off at the mouth.

Or I replay the scene and I give him that cool, calm, and collect Classy B response. *Baby you don't have to put me down to try to impress the new girl. Heck, you lost any chance with her when you started reading in class, Cat in the Hat.* Everybody cracks up, and I still come out on top.

I'll run a scene a-100-times in my head, if I had to, all in search of the perfect comeback. And then from there my imagination takes over and before I know it, I will have acted out my entire life. This usually takes so much of my energy that I wouldn't even be bothered anymore. But today, I'm not in the mood. So, I decide to just stick with ignoring the new girl until that final bell rings to dismiss school.

Under similar circumstances, the day would drag on like a wooden leg in the mud. But luckily for me, the day goes by faster than I anticipated, which is good for me since I still must go over to Mrs. Cooper house to finish the room for her granddaughter. I started on the room on the weekend and I had just found the bed right before leaving. I swear I have never seen so much junk packed in a room before in my life.

As I make my way to Mrs. Cooper's house beads of perspiration form on my head. Normally, I would just take the bus to her house but I'm still trying to avoid any dealings with Desmond. Resulting in me fighting this three o'clock sun that is currently kicking my behind.

Ten minutes later, I arrive at Mrs. Cooper's house out of breath and my shirt drenched with sweat. Usually the front door is open, but today it is closed and locked. I don't panic since I'm one of the two people who knows where the spare key is. I move one of the flowerpots on her front porch to retrieve it. I've been going to Mrs. Cooper's house for so long she really considers me family which means a lot since she doesn't even consider some of her blood relatives' family. Her whole argument is that anyone who steals is no family of hers. Mrs. Cooper has determined that family thieves were probably switched at birth, adopted, or dropped on the head when they were little. If you do steal, then you are labeled as an extension cord. Meaning if you act right you can stay connected with the family, if not… *"I'll unplug that mother *bleep* quicker than quicksand can sank the Titanic."*

I have no idea where she comes up with this stuff. But she's so thrilled with it that you have no doubt she means every bit of what she says. She keeps me rolling. I let myself in and I notice the television is off which is a clear sign Mrs. Cooper isn't at home. I decided to start cleaning even though Mrs. Cooper was not at home. I run to the kitchen for a snack then I headed in the spare bedroom to finish what I had started.

I enter the room and I did a double take. I stand in the doorway; my mouth was wide open. I survey the room which I had been in this past Saturday carefully. The room is a stark contrast to what I saw Saturday.

Practically overnight, Mrs. Cooper had transformed the room into a modern age typical teenage haven. The original décor resembled a miniature library with a bed. Old portraits of Mona Lisa and a white Jesus that were once plastered across the room were now replaced by posters with inspirational quotes on them. One poster written in bold crimson letters, placed in the middle of the wall boldly stated, "The Keys to Happiness and Hope are Already in my Hand." Others expressed inner love like, *"I am Beauty, Beauty is Me"* and *"Fearfully and Wonderfully Made."*

Mirrors of all shapes and sizes were placed on every wall of the bedroom, which was a very stark contrast of my bedroom where I intentionally removed every mirror because I absolutely hate looking at myself. I feel the positive energy as soon as I enter the room. The energy is so powerful, it seeps in my pores, hitting nerves that send shock signals to my brain that give me a 'happy fuzzy feeling.' I am so taken aback by the newly renovated room;

I didn't notice the two eyes peeking from the closet. These eyes happen to belong to Jerica. What in the world is she doing here?

"Oh, hi, I didn't realize you were in there." I stammered, suddenly feeling awkward.

"That's okay. Lillian? Right?" she asked looking at me quizzically.

"Yeah, that's it. But you can call me Lily. I didn't realize that you were Mrs. Cooper's granddaughter. I thought you were coming this weekend."

"Yeah, I was. But some paperwork was pushed faster than we expected which allowed me to get here sooner. So, you are the one my grandma talks about all the time. She has told me so much about you." She stated leaning in to give me a hug.

Clumsily, I pat her back. I always had a problem with letting other people within my space but since she was the granddaughter of the most amazing woman I have ever met, I felt it only right to offer her the gesture back.

"So, how do you like it so far Jerica? New school, new city, new people, it must be a little overwhelming for you?"

"Truth be told, I'm used to being bounced around from one place to another. Now I take it all in stride. I just come into new situations with the mentality of making the most out of it. By the way everyone calls me Jerica."

"Jerica, what you've done to this room is so dope." I was still in awe of the makeover as I walked around the room.

"Thank you. I take these posters everywhere I go. It makes me feel more 'settled', whatever that means." *Everywhere she goes.*

"Where do you buy them?"

"I usually can't find posters with inspirations that fit me, so I make up my own and get them printed up at a print shop. I just like customizing words that empower me. Take this one for instance," pointing to the board written in crimson red letter that I was just admiring, "this is an actual picture of my hand. I had it written in bold crimson because red resembles power and authority and strength. You can find a thousand posters about the keys to success but in my darkest moments I don't seek success, I just seek hope and happiness."

"So, you come up with slogans to help you get through difficult times?" I asked.

"Yes, it's all about putting words into something I can visualize. When I wake up every morning, and the sleep is still heavy on my eyes, the first thing I see is this board. Before the sorrows of yesterday try to flood and overtake my thoughts and my sanity, I see these words. Sometimes I stare at my hand and I can actually see keys. It reminds me that no matter what is going on in my life, no matter how hopeless I may feel, no matter how dark times may be, that God has already given me the keys and it's up to me as to what I do with them." Jerica spoke like a pastor on a Sunday morning television broadcast.

"Okay, I understand the reasons for the posters but what's up with all the mirrors?" I asked curiously. Turning to me she asked, "Why do we have mirrors?"

"To see how we look, I guess." I shrugged unsure of whether this was a trick question.

"Yes, exactly. We must see who we are for us to embrace who we are. There was a time that I didn't want any mirrors around me. I hated looking at myself. I would shy away and duck around corners to avoid them. That's because every time I looked in a mirror, I only saw what's wrong with me. I saw the blemishes on my face, or how I was too big, or what was wrong with my hair, or that I was too short or too tall. But that all changed with a little help from Grandma Coop. She always knows what to do when I need her the most."

"Yeah, and she always knows what to say with that smart mouth of hers. I swear I come by just to see what crazy stuff will come out of her mouth next."

"Girl, you don't have to tell me. You just missed her go off on this dude who was tripping because she didn't have any Newport 100s. She told that fool that he could either buy the short she had or go outside and piece together some cigarettes off the ground and make him a Newport 1000 for all she cared."

Both of us fall out laughing. "I swear that woman has no chill."

"No, she doesn't but she has wisdom for the soul. It is because of her that I am no longer ashamed of who I am. She helped me realize that I'm special when I thought I was a 'nobody.' I use to really think I was ugly because that's what other kids use to call me. Now, I look in the mirror and I see beauty looking back at me. You see this?" she asked pointing to another poster on the wall. It was a closeup picture of Jerica's face and written beside it was 'Beauty lies in the eyes of the beholder.'"

"Grandma taught me that what is considered beautiful is different to different people. Meaning what is beautiful to me may not be beautiful to you. And what looks good to you may be ugly as hell to me. It's all about perception. And since there are over 7 billion people in this world, I had to learn that what I think about myself is the only thing that matters because I would go crazy trying to be something for everybody else, when everybody's perception of beauty is different.

Jerica walks over to her large closet. It was already filled with shoes and clothes. She reached for the top shelf where there was a line of wigs on mannequin heads.

"These are my sisters." Jerica exclaimed while lining the heads on her dresser. "This is Jazzy." She says as she picks up a shoulder length, layered bob wig.

"This is Chen, my Chinese cut bang wig. And this one I named Rhianna. I don't know why but Rhianna has worn some curls like this before. Sometimes when I get tired of wearing my one ponytail, or if I don't feel like flat ironing my hair, I just pull one of my sisters out and they come through for me."

"Your mom lets you wear wigs?" I asked shockingly.

"Well, my mom is not always around so I don't have to get anyone's approval for the most part," Jerica said, her voice full of sadness.

"Let me show you how trying to be what other people consider 'beautiful' will literally send you to the nuthouse." Jerica continues. "This is how I felt before I gave up trying to fit in and please everybody. Here's how it goes. Whenever I say something is wrong with you, you must try to fix it. Take for instance, if I say your hair is too short you must go and pick up a wig that is longer. Got it?"

Unsure about what I was about to do. "Yes, I think I do."

"*Well Lily your hair is so short you can curl it with rice.*" Jerica sneered reciting a poor imitation of Desmond.

Trying to hold back a smile, I reached for Chen and put her on my head. Just as soon as I put her on, Jerica started another horrible imitation of some unknown person. "Girl, why did you grow your hair out so long, you looked way better in shorter hair."

I grabbed Chen off my head and placed her back on the mannequin's head.

"Oh, Lily you are too skinny. You need to eat something skinny bones."

Confused I looked up at Jerica. She was handing me over two pillows pointing them in the direction of my stomach. I grabbed the pillows and stuffed them under my shirt.

"You know that those shoes are so outdated. Your momma must couldn't afford you a pair of real shoes." Jerica was now inside her closet pointing at her shoes.

I reached down at the collection of shoes strategically placed on the closet floor. I picked up a pair of Lebron's which I had been wanting for a while, but my mom refuses to pay $200 dollars for shoes.

I had just gotten them on when I could hear Jerica say, "Oh you think you all that now! Got your first pair of Lebron's and now you think you better than us."

Jerica's mimicking went on for about five more minutes and when she finally finished, I sprawled out on the bed breathing heavily.

"You see how tired you are?" Jerica stood towering above my head. "You see how crazy it is. When you try to satisfy one person, here goes ten more people that comes up with their opinions about what they think you should wear, how big you are supposed to be, how long your hair should be? Then, they decide to pick on you for being different from what they believe you should be. You can never satisfy them all. That's why how you feel about yourself should be more important than anyone else's opinions about you."

I laid there processing everything Jerica said. Looking back over my life, I could see how I let so many people's opinions about me dictate who I had become. I thought about my favorite scrunchie my grandad had bought me that I used to wear all the time until someone said that it was ugly, and I stop wearing it. I remembered my favorite and most comfortable Sketchers I had owned and worn faithfully.

Yet, again I stop wearing them because I was being teased for not having a pair of "name brand shoes." I literally cried every morning until Mom bought me a pair of Nikes. And I can't forget about my glasses I use to love because I thought they made me look like a teacher but now I barely wear because other students were calling me four-eyed. Not to mention, I can't see a thing without them, but my mom thinks I'm too young to wear contacts so now I'm stuck sitting in the front of the class just to see the blackboard.

Suddenly, it dawned on me that I've been so lost in criticism, opinions, and bullying for so long that I really hadn't truly found out who I was. Instead of focusing on what made me happy, I just tried to fit in with everybody else hoping with all hopes that it would satisfy them enough to accept me. But it never has. The heart ache of this rejection keeps me locked away from the world.

Too afraid to be myself. But after tonight with Jerica's help, I can feel a yearning deep inside me to break free. A small flame in a very dark tunnel, but it has given me a newfound hope. Maybe, I can tear down the walls that keep me hidden.

Maybe just maybe, I'm ready to present the true Lillian Mitchell to the world.

CHAPTER 3

Two Plus Two is Six

Jerica invited me over on Saturday just to hang out. I happily agreed since I didn't have any other plans. It has been awhile since I spent my Saturday doing anything other than watching a movie or curled up in my bed wearing my onesie all day reading a book. So, when Jerica asked me what I did for fun on the weekend, I couldn't name one thing.

"You mean to tell me you don't do anything for fun?" Jerica asked wide-eyed in disbelief.

"Well, I do watch movies and read books."

"No, I mean fun. Like going to the movies, or to the mall, the skating rink, or the trampoline park."

"Nope. I really don't like going out much."

"And why is that?" Jerri asked.

Because I don't see a reason to leave the comfort of my house just to go out and let the same kids from school talk about me in public.

"I don't know. I just don't." I lied.

"Why did you just walk away when Desmond called you fat?"

"I don't know, what was I supposed to do? Fight him? I just left. I didn't know what else to do." I said a little annoyed at the fact that she was bringing the situation up.

"But why did you just leave. Did he make you mad? Did he hurt your feelings?"

"Of course, he hurt my feelings. Wouldn't you be hurt if someone called you fat and ugly and humiliated you in front of everybody?" Now, I went from annoyed to angry.

"Let me ask you this. If Desmond would have come to you and said milk is green, a stop sign is blue, and two plus two equals to six would you have gotten mad?"

"No." I would have just thought he was dumber than I thought.

"Why not?" Jerica asked staring me down waiting on me to respond.

"I don't know, I guess because there wouldn't be a reason for me to get mad about something, I know isn't true."

"Okay, if Desmond would have said milk is green you would say?"

"No, milk is white." Unless he was talking about chocolate milk.

"And if he said a stop sign is blue and two plus two is six, you would have responded how?"

"I would've said a stop sign is red and two plus two is four." I said clearly not getting the point of this hypothetical situation.

"And when he said that you were fat and ugly, you could've responded, 'what?'"

Oh, okay. I like how she just did that. "I'm waiting Lily. You could have said what?"

"I guess I could've said I'm beautiful no matter what size I am."

"And that's the problem, you guess. You guess what? You're not even sure if you're beautiful?"

I wanted to lie so bad, but I couldn't.

"Not really."

"And why's that?" Not even giving me a chance to response she quickly came back "Because Desmond says you aren't?"

I couldn't say anything because that's exactly how I felt. How can I think I'm beautiful when it seems like not only Desmond but everybody else thinks the complete opposite? And as if she was reading my thoughts, Jerica said:

Oh, so since it's more than just Desmond who's saying it, it must make it true. Let me tell you something, I don't care if 100 people say 2 plus 2 is six, it still isn't true. And it don't matter how many small-minded people feel like it's right to call you out your name, it doesn't make anything they say any truer. I use to be just like you letting everybody else's opinions make me feel some type of way.

Jerica gazed out the window.

I will never forget the time when I was in the third grade and Maxine Sellers stood in front of the class presenting her science project on bugs. And at the closing of her presentation she looked directly at me and said that she had named her beetle Jerica because it reminded her of someone she knew. I can remember every head turning to look at me, and I remember every finger pointing at me, and all the laughter that cut through me that day.

I had always been picked on, you know, but this time I was hurt more than usual. I felt something break inside me. I cried all the way home. I really didn't have anybody to talk to back then; so, I called Grandma Coop.

She couldn't understand a word I was saying because every time I tried to tell her what was going on, I could feel the same anger, and the same hurt, and the same sadness I felt in that classroom. And I couldn't stop crying no matter how hard I tried. After five or six minutes of me trying to tell her what happened and grandma telling me she can't help me if she doesn't know what happened, I finally got it all out.

For a moment she didn't say anything. Then, Grandma told me to go look in the mirror. And I'm thinking to myself, how in the world is a mirror going to help me? And she asked was I looking in the mirror yet. So, I went into the bathroom and I looked in the mirror.

And she said repeat these words after me.

I am fearfully and wonderfully made.

I looked in that mirror and said, 'I am fearfully and wonderfully made'

Again. That's what she said after I said it. I said it over-and-over again. She made me repeat it at least 20 times while looking at myself in the mirror. And to be real with you, I didn't understand what those words really meant at first but every time I said them, I felt a little better. Every time I said it, I said it a little stronger.

Grandma made my granddad drive her all the way to New

Orleans. I can remember her cooking her famous tea cakes that I love. And while we were eating them, she told me to tell her what happened again.

I told her how I was being bullied and teased every day. And she asked me how it made me feel. And I told her that sometimes I didn't want to live anymore, that the hurt was so much that I could barely take it. I felt like I wanted to trade lives with somebody, I didn't want to be me. And I knew that it was impossible, so that made me feel hopeless. I felt like there was not going to be an end to my sadness, no end to my pain.

Now, it's taking everything in me not to blink, knowing that only one blink will turn on the waterworks and I wouldn't be able to turn it off. And when I say everything, I mean everything. Lauryn Hill's "Killing Me Softly" song lyrics would be nothing short of how I feel at this very moment. "Killing Me Softly" is another great oldie but goodie I've learned thanks to my mom. Jerica was telling my whole life with her words. Every hurt she spoke about I knew personally. Her pain, I felt also. Every ounce of hopelessness that she had experienced was now my everyday life.

Jerica walks over to her dresser and opens a case containing various art supplies: Crayons, markers, scissors, and glue. The case was a kindergartener's dream kit.

"I want you to do this project Grandma made me do. But first let me ask you this, what is the definition of beauty? "Jerica asked.

"I don't know. I guess it's something that is pretty."

"Well, according to Webster, beauty is a combination of qualities, such as shape, color and form that please the aesthetic senses, especially sight. I want you to grab those old magazines from under my bed and we're going to make a collage of all the stuff we think is beautiful."

I pull a dusty container from under the bed. It is filled with the same old Jet, Ebony, and other magazines that Grandma Coop wouldn't let me throw away.

"You're going to do this project Grandma made me do that day. You're going to cut out pictures of people that are beautiful to you."

I grab a magazine and start to thumb through the pages. After ten minutes of cutting and pasting pictures on the construction paper Jerica provided me, I had created a collage of people of all ethnicities. African Americans, Caucasians, Native Americans, Mexicans, Russians. Some were big, some small, some short, some tall. Some were famous. Some I hadn't seen before.

Jerica looked down at my paper and said:

Beauty is qualities that pleases me. That pleases my grandma. That pleases you. That pleases your mom and your neighbors and the people at the grocery stores, and at the movies. Beauty is qualities that satisfies the Maxine Sellers and Desmond's of this world. What looks good to me, may not look good to you. And what looks good to you may not look good to me. But images of people are still beautiful. But, to each its own.

There is no book that says you must be a certain height to be beautiful. No book that says you must be a certain color or have a certain length of hair or must be a certain weight or be of specific backgrounds. Beauty is held differently in the eyes of everyone in this world. We are all beautiful. More importantly, beauty is being fearfully and wonderfully made. The difference in every one of us is what makes us all beautiful. The fact that there is only one of us, makes us beautiful.

***

The morning sun glistened through the closed blinds of my bedroom marking the beginning of the day. I open my eyes to pink, blue, and yellow sticky notes all over my room. Jerica's posters and what they meant to her had inspired me so much that I had come home wanting to write my own words of encouragement the rest of the weekend. Without the fancy printing and artwork that Jerica used, I came up with something creative. The only thing I could find were some sticky notes my mom uses to jot down notes and a grocery list. But the notes did the trick.

The first note I saw when I woke up was *Faith over Fear*. I've heard this statement my whole life but never really understood its meaning until now. I know now that if I'm ever to do anything that really makes me happy, then, I must let go of my fear of people's opinion of me. I must stop being afraid that people may laugh at me if I do certain things or if I wear certain clothes. I should not allow fear to keep me from signing my name to enter the talent show that I want to enter even though I'm too afraid of the negative attention a public stage may bring me. Now, I believe I can overcome everything that held me back over the past few years. From now on nobody's opinion of me will keep me from my destiny.

In fact, today will be the day I sign my name up for the talent show. I will not let anyone prevent me from showing the entire school that I am unique. I once lived behind the shadows of my peers but today I see a light casting out the darkness that has consumed me for too long. I will no longer hide. I will no longer be ashamed. If only I can gather the courage to overcome my fears.

This morning felt incredibly different. Now I knew what Jerica meant when she said that she felt empowered every time she spoke those words in front of the mirror. I had placed my power words all over my bathroom mirror, on my dresser mirror, on the lamps, and anywhere I knew I would look. My notes included sayings like, *don't let them steal your joy, I am somebody*, and before *you find your book bag, find hope.* I knew I would find myself looking for my bag every other morning, and I wanted to reach out and touch and awake the positive feelings hidden in my soul.

I know it's crazy after only a couple of days around Jerica I feel like taking on the world. But, hey, it's a first Sunday in every month. And this is the first time I want to show the world the real me. It's the first time I felt strong and brave enough to fight for my life.

Today, I'm not worried about being the first one at the bus stop.

You can do this Lily. It's no big deal; just get on the bus and do it.

I step on the bus and instead of asking anyone to sit down, I take a seat at the first available opening. It just so happened that the first available seat is occupied by Michelle.

I can't believe I just did that. And from what my peripheral vision is showing me, Michelle can't either.

"I didn't tell you that you could sit down." Michelle sputtered.

"Well the way I see it, this seat does not belong to you. This is property of Langley Middle School district. And until you show me the receipt that proves you purchased this particular seat then I will continue to sit in it."

Slight laughter could be heard throughout the bus. One student yelled out "I guess she told you, Michelle."

Michelle stood up hovering over my head. "Get off my seat or I'll make you."

"If you feeling froggy then, jump Kermit."

I said seriously as I now stood hovering over her. For a moment it appeared that Michelle seemed to want to hit me, but I was a giant over her, and I guess that made her change her mind. She quickly retreated and pushed passed me and found another seat on the bus.

"I don't have to sit with your ugly ass. Why would anyone want to sit with you anyway? Stankin', funky, overweight hog."

I must admit, her words sting. I don't know why I thought they wouldn't. But hey, I'm not going to let it get me down.

I am not defined by what she calls me. I am stronger than words. I will not let words change my mood.

I was focusing so hard on what I was thinking that I tuned out everything and started to visualize me blocking her words. I transformed into Wonder Woman and Michelle was the villain using her words to hurt me, but I deflected every word. I was not about to cry like I normally would when someone says something negative about me. I held my head high. This is a new day.

Michelle's rant only lasted for a few moments. And the laughter that followed quickly died down as well. It was in this moment I realized that I survived the hurt and the pain. I couldn't stop her from saying what she was going to say; but I definitely can change how I react to the negativity and cruelty of my peers.

For a long time, I wished I could be somebody else so I could be accepted. But now I realize I shouldn't want to be anyone other than who I am. And it doesn't matter if people accept me even though life would be easier if they did. The best way to protect myself from people like Michelle is to know that their opinions of me, no matter how hurtful, holds no merit to who I am.

I am the first person to get off the bus when it pulls into Langley Middle School. I practically run the entire way determined to put my name on the sign-up list before I talk myself out it. Dang, the sign-up sheet is gone. It was here yesterday. I'm sure of it because I have walked by it every day wishing I had enough courage to just put my name on it. And to think I was so hyped just a moment before.

I had finally gotten over my fear and was ready to do something I truly wanted to do with no regards of what people were going to say about me. It's crazy how only a couple of days ago, I didn't even want to be noticed now I feel like I lost a $50 gift card to my favorite restaurant. Talking about disappointed. I was so much in my feelings as I walked to my homeroom, I barely noticed Mrs. Myers, the assistant principal, staring at me.

"What's wrong Lillian? You seem bothered."

"Oh, yeah. I thought the last day to sign up for the talent show was Thursday, but I didn't see the signup sheet on the announcement board."

"Yeah, it was but we moved up the date so we could determine how long each act could be. We announced it Friday over the PA."

Must be the Friday I went home early after calling home sick. Karma must be pulling a double shift.

"Were you thinking about entering this year?" Mrs. Myers asked, eyebrows raised in disbelief.

It was no secret I never participated in anything school related. Last year they asked me could I be an extra in one of the school plays. I didn't have any lines just had to stand there with a group of other people. And I still declined.

"Yeah, I wanted to. But next year, I guess."

Mrs. Myers looked at me with compassion and excitement. "I happen to have the list right here with me. If you would like I can put your name on it now!"

"For real? I really appreciate it, Mrs. Myers." Just when I

thought it was over. I guess the world is ready for me after all.

CHAPTER 4

Alley Rescue

I walk over to Jerica's house after school instead of going straight home. A part of me is relieved too because I don't want to see Michelle on the bus this afternoon. From the way she has been staring me down, I'm pretty sure she is still upset about what went down this morning. And to be honest, all that energy I was feeling this morning has worn off. Plus, I want to share the good news with Jerica since she didn't come to school today.

A thunderstorm could be heard leaving in the distance as I strategically walked around small poodles of water. The rain dripping from roof shutters to the sidewalks below sounded like the tapping of drums. I watched raindrops zigzag back and forth across the windshield of cars, parked on the side of the road, searching frantically for another raindrop. And as if each drop had a magnetic attraction to another, the two would intertwine to form one bigger raindrop that sped down the windshield out of sight.

The splashing of the recent fallen rain on the street against car tires going to destinations unknown would be the only sound besides the distant grumbling of thunder belching from the departing storm. Gray skies overlooked the city with an eerie overcast. Usually around this time, the sky would be hued in vibrant red and burnt orange colors as the sun started to descend to the west. The silhouette of birds heading home would add the finishing touch to this artist masterpiece. The usual joggers with their earplugs tucked securely inside their ears, pushing through the final mile of their daily workout were nowhere to be seen.

It was oddly quieter today. Not that the small town was filled bumper to bumper traffic with angry cab drivers yelling out of partially opened windows as you see in New York City. No, the demand of taxicab drivers in this small town hardly seemed reasonable. But over the last few years a few companies could be seen around town offering cab services for the people who didn't want to take the city bus. The sounds of the rustle and bustle of hundreds of people at the intersection on Time Square would be replaced by morning hellos as neighbors go outside to take the garbage out. Discussion of weather, and debates over whether the New England Patriots would make it to the Super Bowl for the fifth consecutive time among a group of old, retired men sitting in the barber shop for their weekly cut would fill the air.

My mind began to wander as the reality of signing up for the talent show settled in. For the other contestants it may have just been the signing of their John Hancock's on a sheet of paper, but for me it meant signing up to give the world a small snippet of who I actually am. Getting on stage means showcasing my deepest emotions through dancing to the entire school. Dancing is easy for me in the privacy of my own bedroom. But now I've signed away my rights to my privacy, forcing me to leave the comfort of the isolated island I had intentionally placed myself for the past few years.

"If you don't give me your slime, I'm going to beat the brakes off you."

I could see a tall, slender, elementary school aged boy

holding the collar of a smaller, frightened boy as I walked by the alley that separated The Quik Stop convenience store and Wok Express, a small, family owned Chinese restaurant that had been here for years.

"I…. I don't have any slime." stammered the boy clutching hard to his book bag.

"If I find that slime anywhere on you, you're going to get it even worse." Letting go of the collar the taller boy began to pull on his mark's book bag.

"Hey what are you doing?" I quickly intervened walking swiftly to get between the two. Startled, he looked around laying angry eyes on me. "None of your business, just getting something that is owed to me."

"Well it looks to me that you are trying to take something that doesn't belong to you." Grabbing hold of the book bag, I nudged myself between the whimpering smaller boy and the bully.

"Didn't I tell you to mind your damn business?" Standing so close, I could feel the heat of his breath directly on my face.

"Say it, don't spray it." I retorted. Daring him to do something about my interference. I stood over two inches taller than him and was at least 50 pounds his senior and wasn't afraid of a physical altercation if it came down to it.

Furiously sizing me up from head to toe, the taller boy took a step back in a sign of surrender. "You better be glad, I don't hit girls. You got my momma to thank for that."

Eyes fixated on me, he stepped back a few more paces and with a quick look over to the still frightened boy that clearly meant until next time, he walked out the alley.

"Are you okay?" I asked handing the book bag back to him. Looking down at the innocent face of the shaking boy. His eyes which were full of fear and sadness now held a glimmer of hope.

"Yeah, I'm alright." the boy replied as he reached into his front pocket and pulled out a small sandwich bag full of a dark purplish substance.

"He didn't get my slime." He smiled victoriously.

"No, he didn't." I found myself smiling as well over this small feat. "What's your name?" He stretched his hand out giving me a firm handshake.

"I'm Julius. Julius Littleton. I swear you couldn't have come at a better time. Jared has a habit of picking on me and taking anything, I get."

"The way you were gripping that book bag, I thought you had something important in it."

"Nah," Julius admiring the bag he held in his hands, "I knew he would think that it would be in there if I acted like I didn't want him to get it."

"You're kind of slick, aren't you?" I asked in admiration.

"Well, I may not be able to beat him physically; but I do have the ups on him mentally. Jared isn't the brightest star in the sky anyway. Fortunately for me." He said flashing me a sly smile.

I found myself smiling again. Julius is small in stature; but he had a big personality.

"Where are you headed, I'll walk you the rest of the way. Just in case Hulk returns. I'm Lily by the way."

"I'm headed home. I was just leaving after school tutorial when Jared saw me from inside the convenience store. The way he bolted out that store you would think he was a bloodsucking vampire and I was his human prey."

Although he said it jokingly, I couldn't help but be emphatic.

46

I know all too well how it feels not to be able to go through daily routines without worrying about someone like Jared making your life a living hell. And for what reason? What prompts bullies to get up in the morning and decide to belittle another person? Does it make them feel good about themselves by making the next person feel bad? And if it does make them feel good, what is wrong with them? It's like pushing an old woman down a flight of stairs. Any decent human would feel awful to even think about doing that. So, what's the difference between me and an old woman? What's the difference between Julius and an old man? Blood flows through their bodies just as it flows through ours. We all have feelings.

We walked in silence until we reached Grandma Cooper's house.

"This is my stop here. How much farther is your house?" I asked.

"I'm just a street over. Will you be walking tomorrow?"

I wasn't planning on it but the way he asked me made me feel like I would disappoint him if I did not agree to walk with him.

"Yeah, maybe I'll see you around then."

"You going to the Candy Lady house?" Julius asks with curiosity.

"Yeah. You want to come in for a few?"

"Yep, I want to see if her house is made of gingerbread?"

"Really, Julius?" I smiled.

"What? Curious minds want to know." Julius shrugged.

I could see Grandma Cooper sitting on the couch from the opened door. I briefly tap and let myself in.

"Hey Mrs. Cooper." I lean over and kiss her cheek. "How

you are doing today?"

"Oh, this old clock still ticking." she said smiling showing off her dentures.

"This is Julius." I said, pointing at Julius. "I want to introduce him to Jerica."

"Ok, as long as he don't have no Spiderman fingers." she said, staring at Julius.

"No ma'am. I'm not kin to Peter Parker. But Denzel is my first cousin once removed as you can tell from my devilish good looks." said Julius, giving her a charming smile while wiggling his eyebrows.

Grandma Cooper chuckled. "Alright, house rule number one. I'll be the only one selling anything around here sir. That means you'll have to start selling those dreams elsewhere, Mr. Washington."

Julius and I both laugh as we head to Jerica's room.

I knock on her door and she lets us in.

"What happened to you today?" I asked as soon as she opened the door.

"Grandma had to finish some paperwork downtown now that I'll be staying here for a while. I suggested that I come along to be her eyes and ears. And to try to keep her from snapping on anybody. Who is this?"

"I'm Julius. Julius Littleton."

"It's nice to meet you." Jerica said.

"No, the pleasure is all mine, My Nubian Queen." he said, grabbing Jerica's hand and kissing it.

Seriously, who raised this boy?

"Can I look around?" Julius asked, his attention now on the posters on the walls.

"Sure." she said, stepping aside allowing Julius to get a closer look.

"What did you do at school today, Lily?"

"Guess who signed up for the talent show?" I said pointing to myself, almost forgetting the reason for coming over in the first place.

"That's good. I didn't know they were having one. I may sign up too. What you plan on doing?"

"I'm thinking about dancing off of Changes by XXXTentacion."

"XX who?" Jerica asked puzzled.

"I seriously think you were living under Patrick's rock before you moved here."

"Just let me hear the song." Jerica said. I pull out my phone and play Changes.

"Whoa, what in the Cardi B - Offset scandal/breakup is this?" Jerica asked after hearing only a few seconds of the song.

"What, you don't like it? How can you not like this song?" I asked.

"I'm not saying I don't like it. It'll be the perfect song if you were trying to win the Miss Debbie Downer award."

"Drum roll please. And the award for Miss Debbie Downer goes to Lily Mitchell," Julius laughed.

The fact that Frick and Frack are laughing at me is not what bothers me. What bothers me is the fact that I literally just met these people.

"Okay, what do you suggest then?" Not even trying to hide my irritation.

"You need something that's meaningful. Something that expresses where you've been and where you are now. It should come from the depths of your soul."

"Yep, just like soul food. I don't eat nothing that don't come from the soul. My girl tried to cook me some nuggets the other day. I was like that's why I need an older woman. Somebody who knows how to feed my stomach and my soul." Julius added.

"Boy, shut up. You too young to know about a girl." Jerica said throwing a pillow at his head.

"No cap. I do have a woman. Now if you want me to drop that zero and make room for a SHERO I can definitely make something happen." Julius said while making his eyebrows go up and down.

"Get'emmmm" I said urging Julius on.

"Lily, please don't give this midget a ladder thinking he can reach any chance of getting with me." Jerica said rolling her eyes.

"Seriously, what do you have in mind?"

"Ok. I was thinking about a song by LeAndria Johnson. It's called Exodus."

Jerica began to sing.

I don't know many gospel songs. But I knew my girl LeAndria. And I swear if I had closed my eyes, I would've believed that she was right here in this very room singing her heart out. Jerica's voice shook me to my core and apparently, she had the same effect on Julius because he sat with his mouth open wide and eyes even wider for the duration of the song.

"Jerica. That was so crazy. I had no idea you can blow girl. I got goose bumps all over." I said rubbing my hands across my arms.

"I know right. Baby girl you just sang my soul right out of my body. Throw me a rope so I can lasso it back in before it goes out the window" Julius threw his make belief rope in a circle over his head for extra measure. Jerica sheepishly looks away from Julius.

"The song has a few voice overs at the beginning that shows how you want God to deliver you from past hurt, abuse, depression. That's where you were. But the second part that says, 'This is my exodus' is your breaking out stage."

"Yeah. Like the Israelites broke out of Egypt and told Pharaoh the hell with slavery." Julius said. Jerica and I both looked back at Julius.

"What? Don't look surprised ladies. I'm God sent just waiting for a lucky girl to receive me." Our incredulous stare did not stop.

"Okay, I was in the Sunshine Band for 5 years and I go to Sunday school faithfully with my grandma. I know a little something about the bible."

"Well this will be your breaking out of the shell you hide in Lily. Let your emotions carry you across that stage. Dance your socks off."

"Yeah, we want to see spirit fingers and spirit toes." Julius said as he ducked his head from the pillows, we both threw at him.

CHAPTER 5

Looking for Trouble

The talent show is less than two weeks away. And I find myself going to Jerica's house to practice more times than not. Plus, Mrs. Myers let Jerica sign up late too since she just started school here. We both critique each other to help with our performance. Julius usually comes over a lot since I've been walking him home every day since meeting him in the alley, even though he spends most of his time aggravating us. He usually makes up for being a nuisance by saying something so dumb we find ourselves laughing and forgetting how annoying he is. Today he had to help his mom around the house which is the only reason why he isn't walking with me to Jerica's house.

I must admit, I'm pretty geeked about the talent show too which comes as a surprise to me because normally I would be scared out of mind. But there's something different about me nowadays. It started off small, like wearing what I wanted to wear without worrying about the opinions of my classmates. Then, I noticed I wasn't looking at the squares that lined the hallways, but I held my head up greeting some of my classmates with a slight nod and a smile. I haven't worked myself up to speaking to any of them yet. But I got to crawl before I walk. One thing I hate more than anything is when you speak to someone and they don't speak back. So, with the head nod they're not technically obligated to speak back which avoids bruising my oh-so sensitive ego.

My friendship with Jerica really helped my transformation. She helped me turn negative thoughts into positive thoughts. Maybe mom was right about the positive effects of being sociable. Jerica is the epitome of a healthy mentally, physically, emotionally, and spiritual middle school girl. But the jury is still out on whether the confidence she holds is because she's considered beautiful or is it because she truly has mastered not giving a flying flip about what other students think about her.

I walk up to the entrance of Grandma Cooper's house. The front door is wide open as usual around this time. It's during the peak of the day and Mrs. Cooper likes to sit and watch the children walk home from school and watch cars with parents headed home from work. I can look clean through the screen door to see Mrs. Cooper sitting on the couch totally engrossed in an episode of Dr. Phil. I let myself in.

"Girl, one of these days you gone meet a bullet walking in my house like that."

"You wouldn't shoot me. If you did who would aggravate you?" I said bending over giving her a kiss on her cheek.

"Nobody. That would be my whole point. Now gone in there and get you something to eat." Running me off so that she can get back into her show. One of the many reasons why I love coming over to Mrs. Cooper. She always keeps a meal or a snack ready. Today she has freshly baked chocolate chip cookies in an old 5-gallon ice cream bucket. That's nothing. You ought to see her McDonald's cup collection.

I grab a handful of cookies and peek into her crock pot to see what she was preparing for dinner: Pot Roast.

"You eating dinner with us?" Grandma Cooper asked as I leave the kitchen and head toward Jerica's room.

"Do you really have to ask?" I retorted and walked out the room.

Jerica's door was cracked slightly open. It was wide enough to see her dancing around with her headphones in her ear and singing in an invisible mic. And singing almost inaudible words. I knew Jerica was being as quiet as possible after Grandma Cooper rudely interrupted our mini NBA Young Boy concert, we were having in Jerica's room last week. Grandma snapped on us like a bucket of snap peas in the summertime.

"I bet you won't unplug those headphones."

"I bet I won't either. I would much rather keep my head attached to my neck." Jerica said jokingly.

"What you been up to?" I asked sprawling across her bed.

"Nothing much. Did a couple of Dubsmash videos that I posted on Instagram."

"Let me see your video." Stretching my hands out motioning for her phone. I always like looking at Jerica's videos. Not that she could do any of the dance moves better than me because I can Molly Wop and Flex with the best of them. We have done some Dubsmash videos together before. But I just like seeing how many likes she gets for her videos. Yeah, I know it may be trivial to some but I can't help but to feel some type of way when she posts her videos and gets 60 odd likes which seems to grow with every new posting as more people from our school start following her.

And whenever I post something, I may get three likes. Four if I'm lucky.

Yes. You heard correctly.

It shouldn't affect my self-esteem one way or another, but it does. I sit and wonder whether I would feel complete if one of my posts get as many likes as Jerica. Will I feel like I have accomplished something? Will I feel important? Popular?

At the rate I'm going, I'll never know. With hope, one day it will never matter. Baby steps Lily, baby steps.

Dang. 42 likes and she just posted the video of her *Millie Walking* in the front of her bedroom window 18 minutes ago.

I scroll down to see who all liked her post. Probably a lot of people from foreign countries I bet. Nah, let me stop hating.

Rodneshia Tate. Antron Robinson. Torrance Chambers. Desmond Snider....

Ugh. I can't stand him. I click on his profile pic that directed me to his page. Let me see what type of stuff this bucket head ninja posts on his page. Ugh. Have I already pointed out the fact that I can't stand him?

I scroll through his page reading and looking at his pictures since I've never had a notion to ever follow him or look him up for that matter.

Can't wait for this talent show Friday. If you wanna see a female WWE wrestler perform, then come to the talent show on Friday... Posted 36 minutes ago...

Is he talking about me? Nah. Then again, who else is he talking about?

"I'm dropping out of the talent show." I said, laying down Jerica's phone on the bed.

Confused Jerica turns to look at me. "Why? What happened?"

"Nothing. I'm just dropping out."

Jerica grabs her phone and looks at it for a moment.

"Why are you even on Desmond's page Lily?"

I couldn't say anything. I really don't know what made me look him up.

"You know if you look for trouble, you better be prepared to find it."

"I wasn't looking for trouble. What you mean?" Now I'm mad. How is she going to turn this crap on me like it's my fault?

"That's exactly what you were looking for. You already know what type of person Desmond is, I don't have to tell you so why put yourself in a position to allow him to hurt you?"

"So, it's my fault that he wrote that stuff about me? So, it's alright that he talks crap about everybody? It's alright that he posts it on Instagram so the world can see what he posts?"

"No, you know damn well I don't condone that crap. But you must take responsibility for what you do. If your skin isn't tough enough to stand the heat, stay out of the kitchen. You are nowhere near where you need to be mentally to go on Desmond page, knowing his history. A lot of people aren't tough to view too much negativity that's why some people, even celebrities don't read comments. Why torture yourself allowing their negativity into your space? Why give it the time of the day? But you had no reason looking on his page, you can't even post a picture or a dance without you worried about who's going to like it."

How did she know that? I never told her that before.

"What? You think I didn't know? You don't think I know that you post the dances that we do together but never posts your own. The reason why I hesitated to give you my phone.

You don't think I know you look at the number of likes I have? I can read you like a book. I post my stuff on Instagram and don't look to see how many people like my stuff. You know why because it doesn't matter. Because what those kids eat don't make me poop. It doesn't matter if one person like my picture. I don't do it for the likes. I do it because I'm feeling myself and if I'm feeling myself, I feel like the world should be graced with my pictures.

Now, what does it look like for me to be feeling myself that much to only post my pictures and then start to feel some type of way because didn't nobody like my stuff. That would mean I'm weak minded. Exactly. And exactly why you don't need to be on social media until you can appreciate who you are without anybody's approval.

You need to deactivate your page until you're ready to post a selfie every day expecting zero likes. Every day until you find yourself realizing that you are still special, you are still beautiful, you are still worthy, you are still somebody even with zero likes. Which is the same thing I did when I got on Instagram."

"I'll be weak minded or whatever else you want to call me. But I'm still not performing at the talent show. I don't want to, and I don't have to."

"So, you gone give up every time somebody say something bad about you?" Jerica asked with a mixture of anger and frustration.

"Look, all this may be easy for you, Black Barbie. But it's different for me. Totally different for me. You get up there and make sure you don't forget the lyrics to your precious song. But I must go there and dance in front of people who don't even want to speak to me. People who don't like me. People who don't hesitate to say some of the meanest things you have ever heard." I retorted.

"Easy. You don't know what I've been through. You think I

got it easy. You have a mom who loves you and cares about you. Do you know where my mom is? No? Me either. You think it's easy for me to know I was brought into this world and not be wanted by the woman who birthed me? Do you think it's easy to hear you whine about how your mom is always on your back about this and that when I would trade a million bucks just to get mines to care at the least? And that's only the tip of the mess of what is called my life."

"I'm sorry about the situation about your mom and all. But it doesn't make anything any better as far as this talent show goes."

"You're sorry? You know what, you're exactly right. You are sorry."

Who does this broad think she is, talking to me like this I think silently?

"Look, Jerica. I don't understand why you're so mad that I'm dropping out of the talent show, but I highly suggest you chill and watch that mouthpiece of yours."

"You'll never understand why I'm so mad because you so blinded by the pity party you always throw whenever things get a little rough."

"Pity party. You think people laughing at me when I step in a room is a pity party? You think walking to school just to avoid the foul things those people say is a pity party?"

"Yeah, it becomes a pity party when you decide to show up at the party. I know you think I don't understand how it feels to be talked about and picked on, but I do. And I'm here to tell you that you will never be able to change what those people think about you. You'll never be able to stop them from saying what they say to you. But you have all the power to decide whether or not you will get down and out and depressed from what the world has to say about you or whether you dig deep and build yourself up and silence the world's chattering and replace it with your own song. The choice is yours."

"Well, I'm not the songbird in this room, Princess." I said giving her a mock curtsey. "Excuse me. I have a party to attend." Grabbing my book bag, I walk out the door.

CHAPTER 6

Sister

It's been two days since I fell out with Jerica: two long, boring days. I hadn't realized how uneventful my life was before Jerica came along. Time always seems to fly by whenever we are together. Just last week, I lost track of time gossiping all day about who's dating who and who's cheating on who. I nearly got grounded for a week for coming in after the streetlights were on. But these last two days have been the total opposite. Instead of time getting away from me, I've watched the day slowly turn into night. The only solace I find is knowing that I still have my buddy Julius to hang out with. Today he asked to hang out with me for a little while before he heads home. And I'll be lying if I say I didn't welcome the company. Even if it was from a mannish, overly talkative, fifth grader.

"Let's cut through the park today." Julius said already crossing the street toward the city park.

I don't mind. Anything to keep me from having to go home. Meadows Park is small with only a swing set, a slide, and a monkey bar. It has a few weathered benches strewn strategically throughout the small lot with a walking trail that surrounds it. A basketball court lies in the northern corner of the park which is the main attraction. The reason why most of the neighborhood kids come in the first place. It's small but it gives many of the children here something to do instead of being cooped up in the house all the time.

"You want me to push you or do you need a lift on the monkey bars?" I ask teasingly.

Julius doesn't respond instead he runs off toward the basketball court as I take a seat on one of the benches. I see some smaller kids swing their legs back and forth on the swings with smiles as big as the horizon. I watch two toddlers hold hands as they run off to their next adventure. No worries. No cares. Just kids whose biggest concern in life is to have as much fun as possible. I can't help but to feel a tinge of jealousy as I long to be caught up in their place of serenity. Thoughts of pure bliss are interrupted as I see somebody walking toward me out the corner of my eye. I turn my head to see Julius but he's not by himself. Who does he have with him?

Jerica. What is she doing here? Even though, I'm happy to see her, I won't be letting her know that.

"Lillian." Jerica says shortly. Greeting me by my government name makes it all too clear that she's still mad at me.

"Jerica." Two can play this game Honey Boo Boo.

"Marco. Polo." Julius chimed in, the only one enjoying himself.

"I thought you brought me here to meet your sister?" Jerica asked angrily.

"Whoa, pump your brakes Judge Judy. I did ask you to come to meet my sister. And I'll introduce you to her if you just hold your horses." Julius is the only 11-year-old boy I know that talks like an 85-year-old man.

"Jerica, this is my sister Lily. Shisshhh." Julius cuts off Jerica before she could argue with him. "Like I was saying, Lily is the closest thing I have to a sister. Jerica, I know you can say the same right?"

Bird chirping silence.

"Okay, I didn't want to have to do this. But clearly you two leave me no choice." Julius looked at both of us shaking his head.

"Sister, you've been on my mind," Julius breaks off in a song.

I vaguely remember hearing the lyrics to the song Julius is now singing in full effect.

"Oh, Sister, we're two of a kind."

I know this Hobbit isn't singing the song from the Color Purple. A movie older than me and definitely older than this midget. The only reason I know this song is because my mom sings to the top of her lungs every time it comes on BET.

Okay at this point I cannot hold it in any longer. Hearing this fool sing would have anybody rolling, me included. But for a second there, I think Jerica is still mad because I don't hear her say anything until I turn around and see her whole body shaking uncontrollable as she let out one of those long, silent laughs.

Before I know it, all three of us are laughing hysterically. I nearly choke from laughing so hard. And that starts up another round of laughter. It isn't until a ball hits Julius that we stop laughing.

"Throw the ball back, stupid."

I recognize the voice before I see whose face it belongs to.

"Can you not hear, or do you not understand, retard?" asked the boy that I saw ganging up on Julius in the alleyway.

Jared.

For a brief, moment, Julius is paralyzed. It's really messed up seeing an outgoing, talkative, boy turn into pure mesh in the presence of a bully like Jared. My heart hurts for him. I just wish I can protect him from people like Jared whose lack of human decency wreaks havoc on innocent people like Julius. And me for that matter.

I open my mouth to give Jared a few choice words when suddenly Julius bends down and throws the ball back over to Jared.

"So, you trying to hit me in the face with the ball, huh?" Jared asks angrily.

Just like a bully who will use anything to start up some mess.

"No, I wasn't. I just returned the ball like you asked." Julius replied.

Before Julius could finish his sentence, Jared is suddenly all in his face.

"Nah, I think you were trying to hit me. So, hit me now. I'm right here." Jared said, pushing Julius so hard he falls to the ground.

Jerica and I both jump up simultaneously to stand in front of Julius separating them.

"Oh, I see you got your big sister here to fight for you again."

"I haven't fought you yet, but you just keep on talking. This may be your lucky day." I say angrily.

Jared steps back with his hand up in the air, "My beef isn't with your big sister. But your boy Julius owes me, and he'll pay up one way or another."

Now the whole park is crowded around us. Some of the kids start to instigate telling Jared to hit Julius.

"No, I'm not going to get him now. Not in front of his sister. She won't let me. But you best believe that she's not going to be around to protect you forever." he said, looking directly at Julius.

Jared turns on his heel and walks over to the basketball court. The crowd begins to clear when they realize that there isn't going to be a fight after all.

I look to see how Julius is doing. Jerica has helped him up and is dusting the dirt off his clothes. I look into his eyes and see tears forming.

"You're going to be alright Julius." I said sympathetically.

"I'm I really, Lily? Because right now I'm not so sure. I don't know what to do. I have never done anything to Jared to make him treat me like he does. So how do I fix something when I don't know how to fix it? I don't stand up for myself because he's bigger than me. I don't say anything to him because I'm scared, he'll beat me up. You know how embarrassed I am? I keep going over in my head, how things can change but I don't see my situation getting better." Julius said, a single tear rolling down his face.

"You need to tell your parents. Get the school involved." Jerica chimed in.

"I've already told my parents. They've been up to the school two times already. And it gets better for a while but then here comes Jared again. I wish we could move but I know that's not going to happen anytime soon. I wish he could just go away and leave me alone. I just don't know what else to do anymore. I feel hopeless." he said, the pain and hurt was overwhelming.

"You don't know what to do? I thought you said you go to Sunday school. Haven't you learned anything from it? When you can't do something, when it's too much for you to handle, when you've told all the people that you love and even, they can't help you, what do you do?" Julius didn't reply but he was looking at Jerica desperate for an answer.

"You pray Julius. You get on your knees and you ask God to help you. You ask God to tell you what to do. You ask God to give you hope when you feel like nothing will work out. And when you pray, you must believe that He can do it and will do it. That's all you have to do."

"Jerica, I'm not old enough to pray. I wouldn't know what to say."

"What you mean, you're not old enough? You think we must be a certain age before we need the good Lord. Grandma taught me a long time ago that the greatest warriors don't fight with their hands, they fight with prayers. There isn't an age limit on praying especially when I know some kids go through as much, if not more, than adults.

Grown-ups are quick to tell us that we are too young to be stressed out by anything. But they fail to realize that most of their problems falls upon us. When money is low and they can't come up with the light bill money, we're all sitting in the dark. We must deal with hunger pains when there is no food in the refrigerator. We go through bullying pains when they can't afford to buy us a decent pair of shoes, not them. And it's worse for us because there isn't anything, we can do about it. We can't go out and get a job because we're too young. Then, they have the nerve to ask us why we have attitudes. Failing to realize our attitudes are a result of disappointments and heartaches our hearts are too young to comprehend.

But prayers let God know that we need Him in our darkest, and most vulnerable times. Believing with every prayer we say, God is listening. But we can't give up, we have to pray through anything we're going through."

Jerica turns to look at me. "And that's what I was trying to tell you Lily. I hate seeing you give up. I just want you to stop giving up so easily on your happiness."

"Preach it, Sister Jerica." Julius said, waving his hand in the air like a deacon in church during testimonial service.

I smile at Julius as Jerica puts him in a headlock. It's good to see him back to his old self again thanks to Jerica. During the last couple of years, I've spent my life feeling hopeless because there was no way I could magically become someone prettier or someone cooler than the students at school. So, I couldn't see the end of my story ending any other way other than despair and pain. But I've accepted this pain for far too long. And that's what Jerica has been trying to express to me.

CHAPTER 7

The Bullies Mom

Ever heard of the expression, *don't let your mouth write a check your butt can't cash?* Well that's exactly what I've done. Being so pissed off with Desmond and Jerica, I marched myself right to Mrs. Myers and told her I wasn't going to be in the talent show after all. If I was thinking right, I could've just not showed up to the talent show at all that way if I had changed my mind (my current situation) I could've still participated. But now I can't since Mrs. Myers gave my spot to the Beta Club. Club leaders were happy for the additional time because they were trying to recruit new members.

Now I'm looking like a long-faced puppy who lost its bone as I head to Jerica's house to watch her rehearse her song. I almost stayed at home, but Mrs. Cooper called and asked if I would pick up some drinks from the corner store. Her customers had to be requesting a lot of drinks if Mrs. Coop is buying them from there since they sell can drinks three times as high as you would get them at any grocery store.

The last time I went to the store with Ms. Coop the clerk asked her, "Do you want your change back?"

She replied, "I don't know what they do overseas in your country but here in the U.S. of A. you don't ask people if they want their change back because we don't ask if you want us to pay for our items."

The clerk declared, "It's only two cents." The way Grandma Coop cut her eyes at that man, you would've thought she was playing Fruit Ninja. As I think back, I'm pretty sure that was the last time Ms. Coop been inside the store which has been well over six months. One thing is for certain, if you rub Ms. Coop the wrong way you will know it because she doesn't have a problem cutting you off.

I push open the door of the corner store and walk into the middle of a warzone. All I see is neck rolling and gum popping.

"I know why y'all come over here in our hood anyway. Making money off us and then try to talk to us any kind of way." a woman with booty length, jumbo box braids was yelling at one of the cashiers behind the counter.

"I'm not, I'm not. I'm just saying you are a dollar short on your money." the cashier said stuttering clearly wanting to avoid an altercation.

I've been coming to this store a long time. I've seen at least eight different set of families run this store. And it's true some of them talk to black men like they are dirt between their toes. But I've also seen a lot of them treat us better than we treat ourselves. So, I have concluded that how people treat you is a personal thing. And the fact that she doesn't have enough money to buy what she wants and trying to turn it into a race thing aggravates me.

"I send my kid up here to spend money with you every day and that's how you act about a funky dollar." The woman said pointing at Jared standing in the corner looking like he was up to no good.

"Money. I have to kick him out the store every day for trying to steal." the cashier retorted.

"You calling my baby a thief? My baby don' have to steal nothing from nobody."

Sounds like a lie. And if she thinks her seed of Chucky is anything like a baby, she may just believe that lie.

So, this is who raised you I think to myself, as I look back and forth from the seed of Chucky to the bride of Chucky. It probably wouldn't do any good to let her know that her son was just at the park terrorizing an innocent boy, and God knows who else only yesterday. I have come across a few parents like her in my short time here on earth. Parents that don't believe or don't want to believe that their child can do any wrong. And if they did any wrong it was surely someone else's fault.

I don't know if it is a generational thing or what but if an adult told my mom something about what I did, she believed them. One time I asked her why she believed what people said without even asking me first. She told me it didn't matter either way because she was going to knock me across my head anyway. First because I probably deserve it for something else, I've done that hasn't come to the light. Secondly, because it served as a not so friendly reminder for me to never do what they were accusing me of in the first place. She was a firm believer in knocking my head off first and asking questions later.

Jared locks eyes with me and give me this *I know I'm no good, but my mom don't care anyway look.* My body starts to tense up. Unconsciously, my jaw clenches and my hand balls into a tight fist. I don't care if I'm bigger and older than him. I just want to smash his face in and knock that smirk off. Let him see how he feels to be on the receiving in of his own bull crap.

I stare him down with pure disgust. I can't stand him. How

does he get away with doing all the low-down things he does? Why does it seem like evil people live their best lives and good people like me and Julius go through hell? It's just unfair and the older I get I'm starting to realize that life is unfair, and we must deal with it the best way we know how.

I try my best to calm down knowing he's not worth me getting upset. Plus, I know his mom would be ready to kick my butt. Maybe, if I'm lucky, I'll catch him when he's alone. I grab the case of drinks before I do something I regret and cut right in front of his mom and put my drinks on the counter. I assume my sudden interruption stuns her since she stops in mid-sentence. The silence makes me uneasy because I have a pretty good feeling that she's staring me down. I decide not to look in her direction. Why should I care when she isn't doing anything but causing an unnecessary scene anyway?

"Little girl, didn't you see I was talking? Didn't your momma teach you any home training?"

My momma always told me to respect my elders, but this is one time I'm willing to risk getting a fist across the lip. But before I can open my mouth, a man walks from the back of the store holding a beer to my rescue.

"Ju-Ju don't start with that little girl. She's a paying customer and don't nobody have no time to sit up here listening to your messy ass all day. You don't have enough money so step aside because I was going to do the same thing if she hadn't beat me to the counter first." the man said.

Ju-Ju swings her head around so fast, I can hear the muscles in her neck pop. She doesn't waste anytime chewing him out. But every time she said something, he had a comeback that made her even angrier. They continue to go back and forth and all I can do is breathe a sigh of relief because there was no telling what I was going to say to her, and I really didn't know how she was going to react. But I did know I didn't want to be posted on Facebook,

Instagram, or World Star Hip Hop if I got into it with this woman. I can only imagine what the heading would say, *Innocent Girl Gets beat up by Angry Mom and her Son.*

Thank you but no thank you. I do not want my name out there like that.

One look at the cashier and I can tell by the way his whole demeanor has changed that I'm not the only one thanking the good Samaritan for the distraction. And with any luck, Ms. Ju-Ju will go on about her business. I pay for the drinks and walk toward the door without looking back toward the two of them as they continue to bicker. I have no intention of waiting to see the outcome.

As I walked to Mrs. Cooper house, I imagined what kind of lifestyle Jared lived. I knew he was a bully but today I find out that he steals and has a drama queen mother. I wonder does she talk to him about doing the right things. I wonder if he has any positive male role models to set an example to show him how to be a man. By the way his mom acts, I wonder does he have anybody to guide him and encourage him? By his behavior I think I know the answer already. So, can I blame Jared for being the product of his environment? Or does everybody have this inner voice to let you know when you are behaving poorly regardless of the circumstances? I go back and forth with my thoughts all the way to Mrs. Cooper's house.

"I'm surprised you didn't roll in here in a wheelchair. I just knew they would've charged you a whole arm and two legs for them drinks." Grandma Coop said looking inside her purse for money to pay me back.

"Nah, just eight fifty." I laugh out loud as I watch her head shoot up to look at me.

"Girl, you better stop playing with me. I was about to send you right back up there to get your money back to tell those fools they had the right plan, but they had the wrong man thinking I

71

was going to pay damn near ten dollars for a case of drinks. Now how much were they really?"

"They were only five dollars." I said truthfully this time.

"Still too much for these off-brand pops. I see if they were the real Colas." she said counting out the money to give me.

I take the money and head to Jerica's room. I can hear Julius voice from outside the closed door. He's over here more than me now.

"Woman, you need to stop playing hard to get. A love like this only happens once in a lifetime. *You better hold on to me. You see I'm a special kind. A man like me is hard to find. I told you a thousand times baby hold on to me.*" Julius began to sing.

"I'm convinced that you are a 45-year-old man trapped in the body of a 12-year-old boy. What do you know about Gerald Levert?" I asked smiling at Julius.

"What I know about Levert?" looking incredulous. "I'm the king of R and B. I'm your neighborhood smooth operator. I'm your lover and friend. I'm your Mr. Wrong."

"No, you're just an annoying little boy who gets on my last nerve." Jerica said.

"Boy? I got your boy."

"Dang, Julius. I need to be practicing for the talent show but all I've been doing for the last thirty minutes is wonder is there an on/off button that I can switch to shut you up."

"Oh, it's like that? That's what you want? I'll leave right now and watch how you'll be begging me to come back."

"Don't let the door hit you where the good Lord split you." Jerica points at the door.

"Don't keep pushing me, woman." said Julius yet he doesn't

72

move an inch.

"Remind me of who introduced me to this minion so I can beat their butt." Jerica says to me.

"What?" I shrugged giving her *I don't know who you are talking about look.*

"You ready to practice on your praise dance?"

"Practice for what, I can't perform so I don't see the point?"

"The point is you should do it because you love dancing. It doesn't matter if you're in a talent show or in your bedroom. If you like dancing, then do yourself a favor by doing it anyway. Audience or no audience." Jerica replied.

"But I don't have..."

"You don't have no excuse, so let me see you shake some, Thotiana." Julius chimes in doing an awful rendition of the song.

I swear after walking with Julius every day after school, I find myself irritated more than usual. He knows I hate that song and he knows I hate it even more when he slides across the floor, throwing imaginary money like he's in a music video. And to make matters worse Jerica jumps up and joins in with him. I can't take it anymore.

"Okay, okay, I'll do my dance just stop singing that song please." They both laugh victoriously. I roll my eyes at them both. Note to self: fire old friends and interview for new friends as soon as possible.

Instead of Jerica playing the song on the computer like she usually does, she starts to sing the lyrics of the song. Her angelic voice vibrates off the wall into my ears as I stood frozen in place amazed at her pure natural talent. It isn't until she stops mid song and gave me a crazy look that I realized she wanted me to dance.

"Oh, you waiting for me to dance?"

Jerica's mouth doesn't open but she gives me a look that says, *what else am I waiting for?*

She starts back up and this time I begin my praise dance. And I must admit it feels really good too. I haven't even attempted to do my dance since I found out I couldn't perform but that didn't matter because I don't skip a beat. Jerica worked on my dance to perfection over the last couple weeks making sure all my moves synced with the words to the song. And from the look on her face, she's well pleased with the results.

"We're going to kill it tomorrow." Jerica said when she finishes the song.

"We? Who is we?" I asked.

Jerica clasped her hand over her mouth like she has just spilled the beans.

"That's what you get. And you were worried about my "big mouth." Julius said using air quotes when he got to big mouth.

"Shut. Up. Julius." Jerica said slowly emphasizing every word. "It's your fault anyway."

"Now how you gone blame this on me? I swear, I can't with you women." he said shaking his head.

"What are you two talking about?" I asked, eager to find out what all the commotion was about.

"Well, we were going to surprise you tomorrow. But since Julius can't seem to keep his mouth shut, I'll tell you now." Jerica says sarcastically, "Since you lost your spot in the talent show, I went to Mrs. Myers and asked if I could enter the competition as a group. And she said yes. You and I will both be performing as a singing/dancing group." Jerica screamed jumping up and down.

"Are you serious?"

Jerica nodded her head.

So many thoughts. So many emotions. I don't know if she realizes it, but Jerica has a buddy for life now. Throughout our entire friendship, though short, Jerica has been my motivator. She always makes me feel like I matter. It's like she's not going to be happy until I become the best version of me. And when I think our friendship can't get any better, she does this. Selflessly going over and beyond to include my happiness in her world once again. I swear this will go down as one of the most memorable days of my life.

CHAPTER 8

What was I Thinking?

Peeking from behind the curtains on the stage, I can see the gymnasium quickly start to fill. I glance around until I find my mom and Mrs. Coop sitting three rows from the front. My palms are sweaty, and I can't keep still. This will be the first time ever performing in front of an audience. I know how disappointed I was when I couldn't participate but I would rather be disappointed than being the nervous wreck I am right now.

Why did I decide to do this in the first place? I feel exactly how I felt when my fifth-grade class went to Medieval Times Amusement park. The whole class decided to ride on the tallest roller coaster in the park. I'm not a fan of heights but staying at the bottom, waiting for who knows how long, by myself isn't appealing either. So, I just go up with my fellow classmates. How bad could it be I thought?

Halfway up the old, raggedy steps I found out firsthand how bad the ride was as I my anxiety reached maximum levels. I began to hyperventilate and should have just turned around and walked back down. But I was too worried about falling if I tried to get pass the long line of people on the narrow staircase on my way down. I was literally stuck between a rock and a narrow place. Up I went with every step imagining all kind of freaky ways I could die. Just to get to the top to face the real terror, the rollercoaster itself, I watch the people in front of me board the monstrosity and I immediately look around for an escape.

Which is what I find myself doing right now - looking for a way out. What is wrong with me thinking I could go through with this? I wonder if Jerica would be mad at me if I disappeared for a little while. But the look on Julius face tells me she won't be mad; she'll be pissed as he swiftly walks toward me.

"I've been looking all over for you. You realize Jerica threatened to kill me if I didn't find you. What you doing out here anyway?"

"Nothing. Just needed to get out of the dressing room for a while." I lie.

"Oh, it was getting a little stuffy with all those people coming in. Lily, I haven't told you this but I'm so proud of you. I know this must be pretty nerve racking but here you are facing your fears head on. I don't know if I could do it myself, to be honest with you. But I really admire you for your bravery."

It's crazy how life forces you into becoming something you're completely not. Here this boy is looking up to me like I'm some kind of hero or something. Little does he know I was ready to slip out the side door and make a run for it only seconds ago. I swear I don't want to go on that stage in front of all these people but after this heart to heart with Julius, how could I not? Whatever inspiration he has received on my behalf will remain intact if I have any say in the matter. So, if it takes me to walk out on this stage scared, then that's what I'll just have to do.

I follow Julius back to the dressing rooms where Jerica is waiting.

"I found her my love just like I said I would. And I told her how much she inspires me just like you told me."

"Let me brush your hair up." Jerica said pointing at one of the vanity benches. "You didn't think I was going to let you get away that easily now did you?" she whispered in my ear.

What? Did she know I was about to dip out on her? Nah, there's no way she could have known.

I turned my head to look at her "What do you mean?" I ask bewildered.

"I could see that you were getting nervous the whole time you were getting dressed."

"So, you sent Julius to lie to me about how brave I was?" I asked haughtily. I just wouldn't imagine that Jerica, of all people, would play games and be deceptive.

"No, I didn't send him to lie to you. He came in looking for you and started telling me how brave you were to perform tonight. Julius knows firsthand how scary this must be for you. I only suggested that he let you know what an impact you made on him."

"And you knew I would feel some type of way if I left."

"I was most definitely counting on it." Jerica smiled.

"I'm sorry I was about to leave without telling you. I want to do this so bad but at the same time I'm scared of what people will think of me. I can't concentrate on the routine because my heart is pounding so loud. I feel like a bloated cloud in this all white pant suit. The list goes on and on Jerica." I said.

"You think I'm not nervous?" Jerica asked, "Maybe not as much as you but I'm not going to back down from what I want to do because of what other people may think. I just push through it. I bet you Beyoncé feels the same type of pressure before going on the stage to perform and she's Bey. Stop thinking you are the only one who gets stage fright. And you aren't big. I hate that you've convinced yourself of that. You're just thick, Lily. If you could just build up enough confidence and embrace the skin, you're in, you would be flaunting around like you know you're thicker than a Snicker and you wouldn't be ashamed. You've let people convince you that something is wrong with you when I happen to know that you are beautiful. I wish you could look in this mirror and see the same radiant and pretty girl I see. Marcus Wilder sees you too."

"Marcus Wilder? What you mean by that?" I asked amused.

"I wasn't going to say anything because I thought you would have noticed by now that Marcus has been shooting his shot at you girl."

"Jerica, what are you talking about? Marcus is only one of the few descent people here at school but that doesn't mean he's trying to holler or anything."

"First of all, Marcus could've flat out asked you to marry him and you wouldn't had caught on to the fact that he likes you. You would've dismissed it as though he was just nice to everybody because he's a decent guy. Second, I remember at least three times he tried to show you he's interested in you, but his intentions went over your head."

"Three times. Really Jerica. I may not know a lot about boys, but I don't think I would be that blind to Marcus undying love for me." I joke.

"One. Michelle asked Marcus to be her stage coordinator, but he turned her down."

"Who in their right mind would want to do anything for Cruella Deville? Michelle is literally the female version of the Grinch who stole Christmas." I retorted.

"I wasn't finish yet. He also turned down three other contestants, yet he offered his service to you when he found out that you had entered in the talent show."

Oh, I didn't know that. "Two. He told you that you were very cute tonight when we first got here. A compliment that went straight over your head because you are so self-conscious about your appearance."

Okay. I must admit that he complimented both Jerica and me. I just thought his compliment toward me was an afterthought just so I wouldn't feel left out after he had told Jerica that she looked nice.

"Three. I know he's into you because he can't keep his eyes off you. Like right now." I start to turn to see if he was really looking when Jerica grabs me by my shoulder.

"You better not turn around and look. He'll know we're talking about him." Jerica muttered under her breath, smiling as though everything was normal.

How weird would that have been to turn around and lock eyes with Marcus? He would have known we were talking about him. And I probably would have freaked him out looking him up and down as if I could figure out if he really was into me all along just by studying him. Like I find myself doing right now as I look at him through the mirror.

And as if she was reading my mind. Jerica slaps my hand. "Stop looking through the mirror too."

Am I so insecure that I really missed all Marcus's subliminal hints? Am I so unhappy with myself and my body that I turn a direct compliment to a mere salutation? I don't know who I am, but I do not like her one bit.

"I never told you any of this because I wanted you to learn to love yourself. Yes, you have changed so much since I first met you. You aren't shy as you use to be. I see how much personality you have. You're kind, and compassionate, and you are so funny. You walk with you head held higher nowadays. And you did that all by yourself. I didn't want to risk telling you that Marcus was into you and you start to feel all good about the way you look because a boy gave you some play. I know too many girls whose whole life came crumbling down whenever that first boy who told them that they were beautiful went on with their lives and on to the next girl. Now those same girls are lost doing all kind of crazy things. Having sex, wearing tight clothes, acting like they're better than the next girl, all them trying to find and maintain that high they got when that first nappy head boy gave them a little attention.

I refuse to let you be one of those girls. You must promise me you won't become one. I don't care if every girl in this school gets a boyfriend and no one asks you out. I need you to know that you are beautiful and special Lily. I don't care if not one person tells you that you got it going on. I need you to know it for yourself. I thought you would have opened your eyes by now. Do you realize that you haven't changed one thing about your outward appearance? You haven't bought any new clothes. You haven't worn your hair any different. You haven't gotten any smaller. The only thing that has changed is your confidence. Even though you may slip back into old thinking habits like you did tonight; but we all do. Yet, you have more confidence in yourself now then you did when I first met you. You are so much happier just being you. That confidence gives you a glow that is hard to go unnoticed. And it's this same confidence that Marcus Wilder is feeling right now. I need you to see your beauty as an inside out thing."

"I know when you're right." Julius said even though neither one of us realized he had been standing there for the entire conversation ear hustling. "Because I had a girl when I was in the third grade that was the prettiest thing, I had ever laid my eyes on, until I met you" he said as he looked to Jerica, giving her a wink. "But whenever I would ask her about anything we had went over in class or world events she would only stare back at me. Now she could talk me ear off for an hour straight about who goes with who and who said what, but anything else would be like talking to a dead horse. I knew then that it doesn't matter how fine you are, if there isn't nothing going on up there in that space between your two ears, then that is an entirely different turn off.

"Boy, what girl have you had in the third grade? Every time I turn around you talking about another one of your so-called girlfriends. I'm starting to believe you're lying." Jerica said accusingly.

"I don't have to lie about no woman...."

So, Marcus is into me. I never looked at him like that but that's not to say that I wouldn't be willing to go out with him. He's not ugly by a long shot, just a tad bit nerdy. I'm more concerned with what the whole 'going out' thing consists of. Does it mean he carries my books to my locker like they do in the movies? Nah, wrong story for all that mushy stuff. Oh, maybe I'll get something for Valentine's Day. That would be cool. A big fluffy bear, some chocolates, and maybe some jewelry. Then, I'll prance around showing everybody what I got and then I would thank Marcus later. He'll just want to come by my crib.

When my mom is gone....

He'll probably want a kiss...

And then....

Oh hell no. In the words of Grandma Cooper, "that dog ain't gone hunt."

I'm good with just having another person I can call friend. A friend who really likes me, I mean really like me. It's a small boost to the morale. Heck, who am I kidding? I feel like another person as I hear Jerica and my name called letting us know we're up next.

CHAPTER 9

Can't Take It Anymore

A huge smile spread across my face as I look at the 3rd place trophy sitting on my nightstand for the hundredth time today. It's not first place but I'm just happy we placed at all. First, second, or third, at the end of the day it didn't matter to me. The mere fact that I went through the whole competition without chickening out is a victory. But a trophy, a whole trophy. That's like butterscotch and fudge on top of sprinkles and gummy bears on my ice cream. Super sweet.

I replay the entire routine over in my head and I can't think of anything we could have done to make our performance better. Jerica sung with so much intensity, I imagine Jesus himself was moved. My movements hit every word precisely. A story unfolded through the whirling of the flowy fabric that twirled effortlessly with every motion I made. As I danced, I could feel something overtake me. I was no longer in a gymnasium performing for a group of strangers worried about what they would think or how I would do. Instead, I found myself releasing years of anxiety and uncertainty as I danced across the stage.

Time had slowed and I could feel every hair on my body start to tingle. I could hear my heartbeat at a slow and steady pace. No longer was I the girl who was afraid. No longer was I the girl who lacked confidence and was unsure of herself.

My transition was that of a caterpillar as it turns into a beautiful butterfly. That's not figuratively speaking either. Jerica told Marcus her vision of how she wanted the stage. And Marcus didn't let her down. He dressed the stage to look like a grassland and had placed butterflies all over the stage. To top it off, he had one of our classmates made a beautiful set of wings for me. I ran offstage to put on as Jerica began to sing the bridge of the song. It was a symbolic representation of the transformation of something old into something new – like the birth of a new creature. And from the standing ovation we received after our performance, our message was accepted by many.

"Knock, knock." my mom knocks on the opened door as she peeks her head in.

"Hey mom, what's up?"

"I just came up because I wanted to congratulate you again on a phenomenal performance yesterday. You really don't know how proud I am of you."

I smiled.

"You know, for a second there I thought maybe you weren't ever going to see you smile again."

"What do you mean?"

"I know you've been going through a rough patch for the last couple of years. I could tell you were depressed, and you felt out of place. I knew you still had problems with some kids teasing you even after I went to the school and talked with your principal. So, I wasn't sure how to help you. But I knew that you needed help. The reason why I'm always asking how your day is and encouraging you to get more involved. You wouldn't know the many nights I've sat and prayed asking the good Lord to help you find your inner strength to help encourage you amid your darkest battles. And one day out of nowhere, I began to see a change in you. It started small but with every passing day, I could tell that you were finally coming to terms with who you are. And now look at you. I want you to look back at this experience and reflect on it whenever you feel defeated, or scared, or lost and know that you are stronger than anything you'll ever face. I love you Lily Bug." she said leaning over embracing me with a hug.

"I love you too, mom."

My phone buzzes on the table. I don't recognize the number, but I decide to answer it anyway.

"Hello."

"Hey, Lillian." a vaguely familiar voice greets me.

"Hey, who's this?"

"This is Marcus. I hope you don't mind but I got your number from Jerica."

I jump up out of the bed. I know this is not my Marcus. Yes. I've already claimed him. Jerica could have given me a heads up though. Ok, Lily just be cool.

"*Who is that?*" my mom asks mouthing the words out without making a sound.

I ignore her as I push her out of the door.

"No, I don't mind. What's up?" I reply as I pace around the room.

"Nothing much. I just wanted to tell you how good your performance was last night."

"Aw, thank you Marcus. That really means a lot."

"I also wanted to tell you that I think you're pretty cool. And was wondering if we could hangout sometimes."

OMG. I can't believe this is really happening. My first conversation on the phone with a boy. And a boy who likes me at that.

"Yeah, that would be cool. I guess I'll see you tomorrow then?" I hurriedly get him off the phone before I start stumbling over my words.

I break into my best Milly Walk around my room as soon as I hang up. No music playing just grooving to the beat of my own drum. And I must say that it sounds pretty good too. For the first time ever, I'm not living in a fantasy life trying to escape my reality. Instead, I'm thinking of things I like to do and want to do. I'm not focusing on all the negative things I don't like about myself. Why would I when I have so many other good qualities to offer?

I've come to realize that life is all about how you choose to live it. I can mope around and be depressed about things I can't change, or I can say enough is enough and make the best out of my situation. The ball is in my court. I can no longer depend on other people's approval to make my life better. If I did, I would be waiting forever. But right now, I am in control of my destiny. And it's about time too because the world has been missing what I have to offer.

I couldn't see it at first but now I realize life is so much more than clothes and shoes. It's more than how many friends I have or don't have. When it comes down to it, I still have purpose here on this earth. And although I may be young, why should I wait to live freer? As a matter of fact, I'm thinking about asking the principal to start a small interest group for students who may be going through the same thing I've been through. I can't possibly be the only kid in the world who feels alone and rejected at times. I don't want another person to go through those feelings when I can be there to listen to their problems when they need a friend to talk to. I want to be to others what Jerica has been to me. It's the least I can do. I can't say life will be easier from now on out, but I do know dark days gets a little brighter when you have someone by your side that knows exactly what you're going through.

The next day at school I'm surprised to see Marcus awaiting my arrival on the outside of the 7th grade hall. He flashes a smile as I approach.

Oh, are those dimples I detect? Yes, small but still dimples. How haven't I realized how cute he is before now? Okay, Lily get yourself together. This may be your first rodeo with a boy and all, but he doesn't need to know it. Just act cool.

"Hey Marcus. You waiting for me?"

"Yeah, I thought I'd wait for you out here. I was wondering if you and Jerica would like to be in my group for the final project in Performing Arts."

"Um, yeah, did you really need to ask? Who else would we want to have on our team? I forgot to tell you how amazing the stage looked yesterday. You are so talented."

"Aw, that was nothing compared to what you and Jerica did up there. I'm lucky to have had the opportunity to work with you all. You two really did your thing. And if you ask me, I thought you two deserved first place."

"It didn't matter what number we placed. I'm just glad I got through it. For a minute there, I was trying to dip out."

"Really? I'm glad you didn't. You may not realize this, but your performance has a lot of people talking. I overheard Rita telling Deshani that she really wanted to sign up. But she was too shame-faced. But she said if you, of all people, who never wanted to be in the spotlight, can overcome your fears, she could too."

"Was it that obvious that I never wanted to participate in

anything?" I asked.

"Girl, when Mrs. Hawthorne told us that we all had to do something in the winter play last year, and you volunteered to be the tree, I knew then what time it was." Marcus said not even attempting to hold back his laughter.

"What? I could have been the best tree ever. Do you know how hard it is to not be able to move or talk for a long period of time? I've concluded that you and Mrs. Hawthorne are both some haters." I said giving him a smile that would land me a spot on a Crest commercial.

I don't know why but I'm completely at ease at this moment. I usually would feel weird or so unsure of myself talking to someone I hardly know especially a boy. But I'm not even thinking about what he's thinks of me. I'm just being me. Sometimes I can be weird. I can even say I'm a little corny. But by the way he's smiling back at me, I don't think that will be a problem.

We continue to walk toward our homeroom class. I'm not even going to lie. I feel like every student is staring at us. But I decide to keep my focus on our conversation. Nothing strange here, just two friends catching up so keep it moving folks.

A couple of students stop me on the way to tell me how good Jerica and I did. I try to take every compliment as if it was nothing, but I really can't contain how good I feel inside. Neither can I contain the smile that is spread across my face. But in all honesty, I really don't want to. I guess I'm so use to being miserable that being happy seems wrong and out of place. But I'm determined to make this feeling my everyday norm.

"I saw you out there, Lillian Mitchell. Looking good."

I turn to see Desmond Snider smirking at me. You ever have someone to say something to you and they're words aren't offensive but how they say the words and how they look at you give you a clear indication that they aren't really complimenting you but really talking about you. Well, this is one of those moments.

"Thanks." I reply dryly.

"Yeah, I saw you rolling around on stage in your white dress. That was very good dancing you did up there." Desmond continued with a smirk spread across his face like he knew something I didn't.

I don't say anything this time around. If it wasn't clear that he was mocking me earlier, it is now. I walk in the classroom hoping to get away from Desmond before he says something embarrassing about me in front of Marcus.

It's still early so Mr. Stone hasn't made it to the classroom. Murmurings of conversations can be heard throughout the room. Typical day, nothing out of the ordinary. A group of my classmates begin to giggle in the back of the room. The commotion made me look back into their direction. I can see them passing the phone around one to another. But as soon as I lock eyes with them, they quickly look away like they've been caught with their hand in the cookie jar, but the laughter continues. *What is that all about?*

Then, I see Michelle and her clique on the other side of the room huddled around her phone. I can hear laughter coming from their group as well. I hold my head down making it seem like I'm into reading the science book laying on my desk but really, I'm concentrating to hear if someone says my name. I don't hear anything but whispering. Too afraid to investigate Michelle's direction directly, I put my elbow on the desk and rest my head on my hand being careful to tilt my head in the direction of Michelle. Cutting my eyes toward Michelle, I lock eyes with her. Yes, they're talking about me. But what's on the phone that has everybody staring at me?

Since I can't muster enough courage to ask them what they're looking at, I sit still at my desk afraid that any kind of movement would draw more attention to me. And as if he was reading my mind, Desmond walks up to me.

"Check this out Lilian. I told you that you were looking good in that all white, didn't I? I knew you would want somebody to take pics of you on that special night." Desmond said walking to me laying his phone down so I could look at the picture.

Something deep down inside of me told me not to look down at his phone. Just ignore him, I told myself. But no matter what the voice in my head said, my eyes scrolled down the phone anyhow. Someone had made a meme with a big woman in a white dress. The caption read "*3rd Place Winner of the Fatshow.*"

For the longest, I have always upheld my mother's saying. *Don't let them see you cry.* But right now, I feel like this will be the day that it will all come crashing down. As the tears swell up, I try to focus on every positive statement, quote, and advice I have ever heard or read. *I am fearfully and wonderfully made. What people think of me is not my business. Beautiful is an inside out job.*

But no matter how beautiful I am or think I am, these humans seem to always tear me down. I try over-and-over again only to be knocked down time and time again. I understand I can't control what people say about me. I know I can only control how I react to people. But how do I smile in sadness? Seriously, how do I hold back these tears and act as though I'm unbothered by their tactics when I feel defeated? And hurt. And broken. And defenseless. And alone.

"That's it. I can't take this anymore." I screamed angrily running out the classroom and out of the school.

The tears that streamed down my face left a trail of hurt and pain that followed me all the way home. I ran upstairs slamming the door behind me, holding my chest as the weight of despair crushed in on me. I moved frantically around the room looking for an escape from all the disappointments, the hurt, the failures, the feeling of inadequacy, from the laughter, from the shame. But nothing I do takes the overwhelming feeling of despair away.

I lay on my bed but I'm restless. I lay on the floor as my tears creates mini puddles. But I can't find peace there. I open my closet door and bury myself under all the clothes that accumulated over the summer in my continued search of solace. Desperately, I try to shield myself from the world. A world once filled with adolescent aspirations, dreams unfolded, and hope, now only unveiled misery and defeat once again.

I run downstairs in search of my last defense against this overwhelming feeling. A hammock laying in an old oak tree I made with my grandfather. I lay down in the hammock without hesitation or fumbling a skill I've mastered over the years. With my eyes closed shut, I watch the sunlight twinkle behind my eyelids. I began to listen to the movements around me. I hear a squirrel scutter across the lawn. Jaybirds can be heard singing lightly across the winds. And for a mere second, I can see a glimpse of the door of serenity that my safe haven has given me so many times over the years. But the door is abruptly shut as the day's event unfold in my head. And just like that the hurt and depression floods back in. And no matter how hard I try, I can't turn it off.

"That's it, I can't take it anymore."

The anger which was so prevalent in those exact words I spoke earlier is now replaced with a sound of surrender. I stand slowly and defeated. The tantrum I had thrown has now completely depleted me of all energy. Walking sluggishly toward the shed house that was once used to hold miscellaneous goods, I begin to think about all the times my grandfather sent me to go and get items he needed for his small projects around the house. Four by fours that were used to remodel the guest bathroom three years ago lined one side of the shed. Handmade shelves holding chalking guns, a hammer, paint brushes of different sizes, and a variety of odds and ends items took their home on the other side.

I continue to walk purposefully to the back of the shed until I reach the last beam. An old tire rests on its side in the exact spot my grandfather had placed it three years ago. We had planned to put up a tire swing in one of the other big oak trees, but he died of a heart attack before that assignment was completed. I reach up and grab a rope that had been perfectly wounded around a rusted nail. The same rope that we were going to use to hang the tire swing.

Reminiscing about all the times I spent in this shed seems like a lifetime ago. A moment in time where the biggest worry I had was hoping the rain didn't interfere with what my grandfather had planned for the day. A lifetime ago when things seemed simpler.

With the rope in hand, I walk outside to stand beside the old oak tree. Lifting my head to the sky, I throw the rope over the thickest branch I could find.

Lifting my head to the sky, I repeat the words I've heard my grandad always say, "Forgive me Lord, my soul is willing, but my flesh is weak."

CHAPTER 10

Not Yet

The day is drearier than a Seattle morning in the springtime. Dark clouds cover a nonexistent sun. Rain drizzles across the way with no sign of letting up. Cars line both sides of the streets. A pearl white hearse sits directly in front of the steps of a church. A bronze sign drilled on the building front announces the entrance of Temperance Church of God in Christ. Two white gloved men dressed in black suits slowly get out the hearse and make their way to the back and opens the hatch. Upon opening, a pearl white casket identical to the hearse could be seen. One of the gloved men takes out the church truck, unfolding it.

Together the gloved pallbearers pull at the foot of the casket. With a firm grip, they picked up the casket and lay it gently on the waiting church truck. A beautiful, red, rose floral arrangement is methodically placed on top of the casket like a cherry on top of an ice cream sundae. The two unnamed men begin to wheel the casket, carefully as precious cargo, toward the front doors that are propped open on both sides.

Lyrics of a gospel song, accompanied by string instruments, can be heard through hidden speakers within the walls of the church. The pulpit is filled with red roses. Some early comers are sparsely seated in pews. Slowly, the two gloved men make their way to the front of the church. Mourners closely follow with tear filled eyes solemnly walking toward the first pews designated for the family. The left side of each of the mourner's dresses and suits was the home of a single rose. The church quickly fills to capacity as everybody gathers inside. Inaudible whimpering soon grows louder as a woman cries out from the back of the church. Two ushers wearing all white stride toward the mourning woman consoling her and ultimately leading her out the church doors. Her cries, now turned into shrieks of pain, can still be heard behind closed doors. The pall bearers sit on the side pew turning the service over to the church.

The Mistress of Ceremony walks to the podium. Only the sound of paper flipping could be heard as the funeral party retrieve their obituaries. The Mistress of Ceremony begins to read in a clear and articulate voice:

Homegoing Celebration
for
Julius Littleton
on this day of
November 5th, 2019
at Temperance Church of God of Christ

The voice of the MC fades at the mention of Julius's name. The feeling is so surreal sitting in a church saying my final goodbye to my friend. I haven't attended a funeral since my grandad passed away which was a very tough day for me. I can still see my mom crying and I can remember all too well how helpless I felt for not being able to comfort her. I can remember the finality of it all as I thought about all the sweet memories we shared over the years. Knowing I would no longer be able to sneak out the house for ice cream in the wee hours of the night. Knowing I wouldn't be able to hear his deep baritone laughter echo throughout the house as we watched The Steve Harvey show. Knowing I wouldn't see the gentle smile in his eyes whenever he told me he was proud of me, which was more often, than not.

Somehow, I thought it would be easier to say my goodbyes to someone I haven't known for long. But as I sit here, I realize the hurt is still as strong. A different hurt. But still hurt, nevertheless. Instead of reminiscing over memories shared between Julius and me, my heart aches from stolen moments that are never to come. I can remember Julius anticipation of going to see the new Marvel movie. I had agreed to go with him when it come out as he went on and on telling me why Marvel's female superhero was going to outshine DC's Wonder Woman. He was more of a Marvel fan than I. A movie night, never to come.

Or how excited he was to be going to the Spring Gala with Jerica. His mom rented a suit for the special occasion. Julius called Jerica afterward telling her not to change her dress color. He secretly told me that he planned on bragging about having a girlfriend in the 7th grade unbeknownst to Jerica. His stolen night of dancing and laughter never to come.

I know the pain is mutually shared as Jerica reaches over and squeezes my hand. The hurt that filled both of our eyes spoke unspeakable words.

A group of students wearing shirts with Julius's picture on them stood up. Refocusing my attention, I see one of the girls leave the pew and approach the podium as the MC lowers the microphone so it could reach her mouth. She presents the Resolution of Respect on behalf of Julius's 5th grade class.

The girl walks to the front of the pew handing over a plaque to who I assume is Julius's mom since I haven't had the chance to meet her. Suddenly, a small commotion arises as two men help his mom stand up, both standing closely on the side of her as if they were afraid, she would pass out at any giving moment.

Holding a small, red book to her chest, she walks to the podium. She stands silently for a moment as she gathers her composure to speak.

"Hello, as many of you may already know, I'm Julius's Mom." Her voice is low and stricken with pain.

I decided to speak to you all about a side of Julius that many of you may have not known about. We all know how charming he could be. He could make anyone laugh. Most of the time he'd be running his mouth because he could hold a conversation with anyone. He was one of a kind. I use to always tell him he was reincarnated from a previous lifetime. I don't have to go into much detail about that side of him. But what a lot of people didn't know was the hurt behind every joke he cracked. No one knew he had to laugh to keep from crying.

Some of you don't know he was bullied a lot. You may not know how much sorrow he harbored inside because of it. But in the past few weeks, I noticed a change in Julius. He was different. He was more confident. I didn't know what had changed but I was grateful for it. It wasn't until going through some of his things, I ran across this journal. And after reading it, I found out the reason for his sudden change. He had found a beacon of hope. Someone that could relate to him. Someone who understood him on a level that didn't come across so easily for me.

She paused briefly; then, she bowed her head.

"I want to read his final journal entry to you." Clearing her throat, she proceeded to read from the red book.

Today is Halloween and I thought I would be celebrating one of my favorite holidays by dressing up in my scariest costume. Collecting as much candy as I can, picking out all the chocolate pieces to eat first. Instead, I found myself face to face with the one person I wished I could never see again.

My darling Lily you have made me so happy these last few weeks. The day you rescued me from the alley was a turning point for me. I found a friend who saw pass the wall of jokes and charm I hid behind. I thank you for the being a bright light in my dark world. I don't know where you were today when I needed you to rescue me again. But I realize I can't expect you to always be there for me. You have your own life to live. And I have mine.

Til we meet again Sis.

Julius mom closes the red journal and looks out in the audience. "I personally thank you Lily for coming into my son's life and forever changing it. Giving him hope in times of hopelessness. Giving him something to live for these last couple of months. Although at the end, regretfully, he still felt like he didn't have a choice. Yet, I'm comforted by knowing he truly experienced life for the good. If not only for a little while. And I owe that all to Lily. A true friend that helped Julius when he needed it the most. Lily, will you come up and say a few words?" Julius's mom asked as she scanned the audience looking for me.

I had been told that she would ask this thing of me. But nothing could prepare me for it. The day Julius took his life was the day I ran home attempting to run away from my own darkness. That was the day that Desmond Snider passed around that horrible meme of me. It was this very day that my own hurt and sadness overtook me. The day I thought about taking my own life. The day I forgot about Julius. The day that Jared decided to come and make good on his promise. The day I didn't walk Julius home.

Jerica gently squeezed my hand again and stood up knowing all too well the burden of guilt I held inside. I didn't want to stand up in front of these people knowing I had let Julius down. I should have been there for him.

Slowly, hand and hand with Jerica, I made my way to the podium looking at the closed casket that held my little brother. Never to laugh again. Never to smile again. I stood there staring at that casket for what seemed an eternity. Wishing, hoping, wondering if only I was there that day would Julius still be here with us? Arms hugging my shoulders jolted me out-of-my-trance.

"Are you able to do this?" Jerica asked with concern on her face.
"I have to do this for Julius." I reply.

I extend my hand to give Julius's mom a handshake as I reached the podium, but she embraces me with a hug instead as she thanked me for what I had done for Julius. The guilt of knowing that I wasn't there when he needed me the most while his mom thanked me almost made me break out in tears. But I had cried everyday ever since getting the news that he had taken his own life. I don't think I have a single tear left.

With a deep breath, I speak in the microphone.

I met Julius two months ago in an alley. We became friends instantly. He would always tell me that I rescued him that day. But what he didn't realize was that he rescued me. I never would have thought having Julius look up to me would motivate me to be a better person. There was a time that I wanted so desperately to give up, but I didn't want to give up in front of him. There was no time for pity parties and insecurities because I was afraid that if he saw me give up, then, he would too. How I wanted him to see me, pushed me into being more confident, more courageous, and more outgoing. Even when I was afraid. I chose to put fear beneath me because I didn't want him to be afraid. When I was about to walk off stage at my school's talent show, I looked at Julius and immediately I knew it wasn't an option. I didn't want to quit because I didn't want him to quit anything he really wanted to do.

On the journey of becoming who I am, I had Julius to thank for being my constant angel on my shoulder. Always looking up to see what I would do, and I was determined not to let him down. But on the day, he left us, I did let him down. That day I allowed someone to take my joy. I allowed someone to take my peace. I allowed someone to take me out of character so much that I forgot about walking Julius home. Our daily walk which started when I stopped a bully from messing with him the first day, I met him. I saw a reflection of myself every time I looked at Julius. I met a good friend around the same time I met Julius." I look back at Jerica and give her a smile. "And everything she poured into me, I wanted to pour into Julius. I wanted to see him happier and living life with no regrets."

"Oh, God, it's my fault. It's my fault you're not here."

A cry could be heard throughout the church. I look to see where it was coming from. And I lock eyes with Desmond Snider. The hurt and guilt in his eyes was louder than anything he was crying out. *What was he doing here?* Still not understanding, I see Julius mom trying to console him. I looked down on the podium at the MC's opened obituary. I scan down the page and there it was.

Those left to cherish his memories are his mother, Gwendolyn Snider-Littleton, father, Joseph Littleton, and brother, Desmond Snider...

Desmond Snider was the brother to my little brother. It couldn't be. How could it be? How didn't I know? The images of that day flooded my mind. The horrendous meme plastered on all the phones of the students in my class, Desmond's sneer. Me running home. The rope. Julius. It was all Desmond's fault.

"I'm sorry. Julius. I'm so, so sorry." Desmond continued to cry out like a wounded animal. I couldn't blame him. How could I? The pain I heard with every outburst wouldn't allow me to.

Finally, Desmond sobbing subsided enough for me to continue. I looked out to the audience. My gaze rested on Julius's classmates. I knew what I had to say.

My time spent with Julius was filled with life lessons. Things that I would pass down to him that I thought would make life easier for him. Things that would better him. I didn't get the chance to give him a lesson on October 31st. So, I only find it befitting to pass it along to you. I know that for some of you, life is hard. I know that some of you are in a constant battle everyday of your lives. A battle to fit in. A battle to be accepted and liked. A battle to come to terms with who you really are and embracing that person even though you may think you are not good enough, not pretty enough, not smart enough. We can all see our flaws so clearly but to see the beauty that we all hold inside of us is an everyday battle. We sometimes feel that the battle is not worth fighting anymore.

We want to just throw in the towel. Give up. Give up on life. But I'm here to tell you that you can't give up. No matter how hard it gets. No matter how gloomy it looks. You must live to fight another day. And I'm not just saying it, I mean you really must put on your boxing gloves and fight for your happiness. Fight for the freedom to be yourself. Fight your way through disappointments and heartaches. We cannot bear another funeral. We cannot put another father, mother, sister, brother, or friend through all the crying and sadness we're experiencing as we say our goodbyes to Julius. Today I want to dedicate this song to all of you. It's a song by Donnie McClurkin called Not Yet. The lyrics goes like this:

I can't die right now,
I have work to do,
I got away somehow,

Jesus it's because of you
Heaven can wait for me,
I got a destiny,
I got victory
Because God said, Not yet.

Jerica grabs the mic and begin to belch out the lyrics to the song like every word was her lifeline and I begin my praise dance. My final dance for my good friend. I look out into the standing congregation and watch as they sing along with Jerica. Most held Julius's obituary high above their heads. His classmates standing hand in hand moves left to right with the tempo of the song. Some of them consoling the other as they shed tears over the loss of their classmate. Julius's mom walks to the front of the church and stares at the casket that will now be the final resting place of her son. With her held hung low, she leans over with her arms outstretch and hugs the casket. Her tear-stricken face plants kisses all over the top of it leaving a trail of ruby red lipstick smudges all over. The same men who accompanied her earlier tries to gently but forcibly move her away from Julius's casket as she cries out Julius's name over-and-over again. A not so easy task. But after much effort, Julius's mom is led toward the back of the church.

With my eyes fixated on Desmond, I watch him cry uncontrollably as he stares at Julius's casket. His sullen despair is mutually shared. But I can only imagine how it feels to lose a sibling. And as if he feels me probing his thoughts somehow, he suddenly raises his head and locks eyes with me. Desmond has been my arch nemesis for as long as I can remember. But to see him in such pain and agony is something I've never seen. I'm honestly having a hard time trying to sort out my feelings. A little part of me still hates him for the years of torment he's caused me. But right here, right now as I witness firsthand his fragility, his humanness, I am empathetic, like the way I felt when I met his brother in the alley. Now that's some irony.

So, now I'm forced into doing a self-check, a moral check to determine whether I still have integrity and decency or has the exposure to a cruel, toxic world contaminated me to the point that I have one foot inside the door of hell. My last self-check occurred a few months back in the bathroom between classes, when Michelle turns to me ask if there was anything on her face. In the matter of seconds, two responses presented themselves to me in the form of an angel with a halo on one shoulder and the devil with horns on the other. The angel response was a simple no while the devil suggested an alternative response of: 'no,' nothing other than all the speedbumps on your face. After a moment of slight hesitation, I'm happy to announce I passed.

I watch as Desmond suddenly turns in my direction. His steps are slow and fidgety but like a stone his eyes never move its focus from me. And for the very first time ever looking into his eyes, I don't see condemnation or disgust but remorse. His mouth opens and closes, trying to find the words to say, but nothing comes out and he stands before me in complete silence. Another onceover of Desmond and I knew once again I passed yet another self-check as I clinch my arms around his neck, embracing him with a warm, comforting hug. I can feel his tears soak through my blouse. And as if we had been friends for a lifetime we cry together.

Hey Julius,

I reminisce on all the good memories we've shared. And I'm still wondering why you're gone? You don't know about all the sleepless nights I've had wishing you were still here? Everybody misses you. Jerica, your parents and your brother included. We continue day after day but without you our lives will never be the same.

We visited your grave on today. Me, Jerica, your brother, and Jared. Yes, Jared. He came up to me one day after your funeral and he was very remorseful. Feeling completely responsible for your death, he was having a pretty hard time coping with things. And even though I had a hard time even looking at him after all he put you through, I realized it was a lot for him, being so young, to carry the guilt of your death on his shoulders.

So, we talked for a while and I realized that Jared is an alright kid. He too had been bullied and when someone hurt him, he turned around and hurt you. Although it was wrong, it was the only way he knew how to deal with his feelings. And that's when I realized that I had to do something. In fact, we started the YANA group (You Are Not Alone). We knew there had to be more kids going through similar situations just like yours and Jared.

We provide a safe haven to students to talk about some of the things they're going through with Jared leading a lot of the discussions about how he became a bully. We also hang out together just like you, Jerica, and I use to. We just try to make children see that no matter what their situations are, they are not alone. I wish you could have realized that you were not alone before you left us.

Missing You Dearly,

Your Darling Lily

ABOUT THE AUTHOR

Malesha Smith, born in 1984, grew up in the small, rural town of Lexington, in the Mississippi Delta. Malesha used writing as a defense mechanism when she was struggling with self-esteem and depression. Malesha was a member of her high school theatre arts team; she wrote and performed in numerous plays and short skits at school and in her community. Between working full time as a technologist and being a mother of five young children, Malesha Smith found time to pursue her lifelong passion of writing. *Lily Darling*, a novella, is her first work.